W9-CTG-938

The St. Andrews Werewolf

60 YEARS IN CANADA
19 33
19 93

HarperCollins

Other books by Eric Wilson

The Tom and Liz Austen Mysteries

Also available by Eric Wilson

The St. Andrews Werewolf

A Liz Austen Mystery

by

Eric Wilson

HarperCollins*Publishers*Ltd

As in his other mysteries, Eric Wilson writes here about imaginary people in a real landscape.

First Edition

Canadian Cataloguing in Publication Data

Wilson, Eric
   The St. Andrews werewolf

(A Liz Austen mystery)
ISBN 0-00-223906-X

I. Title. II. Series: Wilson, Eric. A Liz Austen mystery.

PS8595.I47S34 1993   jC813'.54   C92-095778-1
PZ7.W45Sa 1993

93 94 95 96 97 98 99 ❖ RRD 10 9 8 7 6 5 4 3 2 1

This book is for "de la"
and it's for every Emily and Wallace

Acknowledgments

The author would like to thank the following specialists in the field of child sexual abuse who so generously found time to comment on this story:

John Betts, counsellor, Victoria, B.C.
Carol Ann Probert, Victoria Child Sexual Abuse Society
Catherine Hudek, Winnipeg Child and Family Services
Donna Harris, Outreach Abuse Prevention, Oshawa
Jacquelyn Jay, Toronto Hospital for Sick Children
Adeena Lungen and Lynne Parisien, Vancouver Incest and
    Sexual Abuse Centre
Peter Balcom, The Nova Scotia Hospital, Dartmouth
Brenda M. Knight, psychologist, private practice, Vancouver
Eveline de Koning, Mental Health Centre, Port Hardy, B.C.
Dayle Raine, Royal Ottawa Health Care Group
Correna Carter, counsellor, Sooke, B.C.
Peter Ringrose, Public Legal Information Association of
    Newfoundland

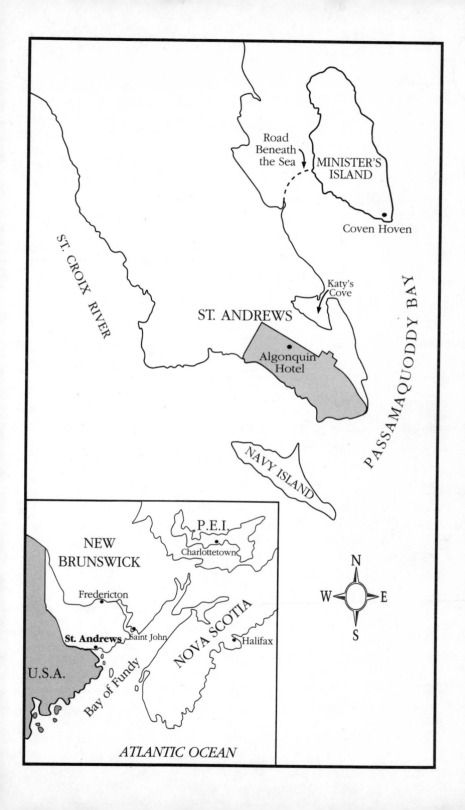

1

"Beware the moon."

I looked at it glowing above, vivid in the starry night. I spun three times on my heel and touched my right ear. "Graveyard monsters roam on nights like this," I said to the woman beside me.

Her name was Fran, and I was her guest for the summer in St. Andrews, New Brunswick. She was a childhood friend of my Mom's. Fran owned some seaside cabins that she rented to tourists. With real generosity, she had helped me get a role in the local stage production of the musical *Annie* and offered me the free use of a cabin.

"You're afraid of monsters?" Fran asked. "But you seem brave, and, I understand, you are a very good detective, too."

"Some things just give me the creeps, Fran. I can't help it! Besides, I am *slightly* superstitious."

"But *you* suggested this walk, just to see the Burying Ground. It doesn't add up."

"I can't resist, Fran. I love mysteries and mysterious places. You told me the town cemetery is hundreds of years old, right? It's called the Loyalist Burying Ground, right? Which means it's ancient, and full of old tombstones and maybe some ghosts. I've got to see it, just to satisfy my curiosity."

"You know what they say. Curiosity killed . . ."

I raised my hand. "I've heard that one before."

She chuckled. "I'm glad you're here, Liz."

I'd liked Fran from the moment we met at the airport in nearby Saint John. She's fifty, with big eyes, and hair that's beginning to streak with white. I like her style and the confidence she has in herself.

Driving to St. Andrews, Fran told some amazing stories. Like the one about last winter in New Zealand, when she was in a chopper that power-dove into the mouth of a volcano. Next summer, she's going north to search for artifacts with a team from the University of New Brunswick.

I fell in love with St. Andrews immediately. Only a few thousand people live in the town, which is sometimes called St. Andrews-by-the-Sea. The first settlers arrived when the War of Independence broke out south of the border. They didn't want to be part of the American revolution. Some brought their houses on barges, and a few actually had slaves. They were called Loyalists, and they were so loyal to the English monarch that they named thirteen of their streets after the kids of King George III and Queen Charlotte.

As we walked through town, I glanced at some of the lovely old houses and churches that lined the sixty perfect blocks laid out by the Loyalists. I felt as if I was starring in *Gone With the Wind*.

"Fran," I said, "what are the signs in people's yards? Some say YES: MALL and some MALL: NO WAY. So far, I've counted seven YES and five NO WAY."

"There's a big argument happening here, Liz. You see all the heritage houses? Well, some people don't want anything changed. They're fighting to protect the charm of our town."

"From what?"

"A company wants to build a big mall at the north end of town. We're talking about a huge place, with hundreds of stores and an indoor amusement park like at the West Edmonton Mall. The mall would have a Loyalist period theme. I heard that they plan to call the triple-loop roller coaster the Paul Revere Rocket."

"Sounds great! Tourists would probably come a long way."

"That's the idea, Liz. There'd be a hotel, and a marina for yachts. Money would pour into town. There'd be lots of jobs for the locals."

"Then why the NO WAY signs?"

"Our postcard-perfect town could become an eyesore. In Maine, some towns like this have become a tourist haven, with Kandy Korner shops, mini-golf, traffic jams, polluted water—the whole bit."

"I see what you mean. The charm of this place would be ruined!"

"Not just the charm, but a whole quiet way of life. A new bylaw has been proposed that would allow the mall to be built."

"I figure you're against the mall, Fran. Correct?"

She nodded. "Absolutely! But only the members of the Civic Trust get to vote. The Trust is a small group of citizens with the task of protecting our town's heritage values. They'll vote next week."

"How's it likely to come out?" I asked. "Have any polls been done?"

"It seemed at first that the bylaw might be defeated, but now it seems that the vote'll be close. Some people on the Civic Trust are in a terrible dilemma. They're against the mall, but have family members who desperately need work."

"That's going to be some difficult decision. I'm glad to be here for the drama!" I smiled at Fran. "It's great talking to you."

"To you, too. I always enjoy a good conversation," Fran replied with a wink as we strolled, enjoying the warm summer night.

"Look," I exclaimed. "That's got to be the Burying Ground!"

Trees grew high above the old graveyard, throwing dark shadows across the tombstones that leaned in every direction, like teeth in a dentist's nightmare. There was moss and tangled grass, and a spiked fence.

A feeling of fear washed over me. "I've seen it," I said. "Let's go home."

"Sounds good to me," Fran replied, turning around. "I'll fix us hot chocolate."

"Yikes!" I stared at the old cemetery. "I just saw some kind of monster!" I pointed to a patch of moonlight among the trees. Something bolted through it. In the darkness, it looked like some kind of large animal, but it ran on two legs, not four. "Come on," I whispered, "let's find out what it is."

We opened the metal gate of the cemetery and moved cautiously down a path between the graves. My heart was doing triple time. I strained my eyes against the darkness. Among the trees, I sensed a presence, something that was alive.

"Maybe . . ." My voice trembled. "Maybe . . ."

Then I heard it. An unearthly sound. Starting as a low cry, it rose to a long, low sound like a terrible moaning. It made my hair stand on end.

Fran and I stared at each other.

"What was *that*?" we both cried.

The moaning died down. For a brief moment, all was quiet.

"Fran, look! Across the cemetery!"

I could see the creature watching us from the dark cover of the trees. All I could make out was its hulking shape.

"It's some sort of creature, half-man, half-animal," I screamed. "I'm sure of it!"

"It can't be, Liz." Fran took a few paces forward, trying to see into the shadows.

"Didn't you hear the sound it made?"

Before Fran could reply, the creature sprang into the deep shadows and was gone. "Come on, Fran," I cried. "Let's follow it!"

Racing past tombstones and bushes, we crossed the Burying Ground and reached the shadowed trees. There was no sign of the creature. Beyond the graveyard, I could see moonlight on a street of homes with big yards.

Lights glowed softly in all the houses but one. It stood close to us, beside the Burying Ground.

"Is that an abandoned house?" I asked Fran.

She nodded.

"Maybe the creature's hiding inside," I suggested.

We dashed toward the door of the abandoned house. Suddenly, a ball of fire exploded out of a window, sending us fleeing to the road for safety. Flames began licking up the wall.

"We've got to call 911!" Fran exclaimed. "The arsonist has struck again."

"Arsonist?"

"Yes . . . I haven't had a chance to . . ."

Just then, we heard an engine start and saw an old van pull out from behind the burning house and disappear. Behind it was a small trailer. The left tail-light was out.

Fran raced to the nearest house. I waited on the street, watching the fire take hold on one side of the house. In the upper window, I noticed a cat trapped inside.

I ran swiftly to the house. The door was slightly ajar and opened easily. Smoke was spreading in clouds across the entire ceiling. Covering my nose with my jacket, I ran up the stairs fast and searched for the cat. It was sticking its nose out a crack in the window for air, meowing.

Grabbing it up, I opened the window. Smoke rushed past me into the night. As sirens wailed in the distance, I climbed down a sturdy rose-trellis to the ground. People were running to watch the fire, some of them in dressing gowns.

The cat squirmed out of my arms and ran into the night.

"Thank you for rescuing that kitty," a woman said to me. She had a soft voice and a gentle face. Standing next to her was a dark-haired young girl.

"Emily and I were out walking when the fire started. We saw the kitty, but we didn't know what to do. We felt so helpless. We both love cats." She touched her daughter's hair.

"You're in the musical with me, aren't you?" I asked the girl. "I saw you at the cast meeting today."

Emily nodded and moved closer to her mother.

"I heard you singing. You are truly excellent." I grinned at her.

Emily smiled shyly. Her large eyes looked at me, but she didn't say anything.

Her mother stared at her watch. "Oh goodness, look at the time! We'll be in trouble at home with my husband. We're late. Come, Emily."

"Good night," Emily said quietly. "Thank you for rescuing the poor little kitty."

"It's safe now," I said.

I watched Emily hurry away with her mother. I felt an ache inside my stomach. There seemed to be a real sadness in Emily.

By now, a big crowd had gathered to watch the fire. I searched through the mass of people, looking for Fran, and found her talking to a man with a kind face, horn-rimmed glasses and thinning brown hair. He smiled at me. I recognized him from the big meeting we had at the theater for all the cast and crew.

"You're acting in *Annie*, aren't you?" I asked.

"That's right. I play FDR. That's short for Franklin Delano Roosevelt, the thirty-second president of the United States. He often summered near here." He extended his hand. "My name is Arthur Dodge, but you can call me FDR. It helps me stay in character."

"Thanks," I said. "I'm kind of nervous about the first rehearsal. This is my first big show."

FDR smiled. "I'm sure you'll do just fine." He turned to Fran. "As I was saying, you have a point. But I wouldn't be so quick to jump to conclusions."

"This is the third fire in two weeks. It's horrendous."

"I'm sure the police are investigating it. If you'll excuse me, I have things to do."

Fran watched as FDR wandered away from the crowd. I was about to ask her to tell me more about the arsonist, when something caught my eye.

"Talk about lifestyles of the rich and famous!"

A black limousine came out of the night, and glided toward the fire. Police officers saluted the limo as it purred to a stop. I went closer, watching as a smoky glass window slid down. Inside was a distinguished-looking man about sixty. What little hair he had on his head was grey and neatly clipped. On his upper lip, he wore a bristly, grey moustache. His eyes were large and intelligent. He studied the fire for a moment, then ordered his driver to move on.

The long, black car disappeared into the night.

2

We told the police everything we knew. While we watched the fire fighters at work, Fran told me that there had been a series of arsons in St. Andrews recently, and some people believed they were tied somehow to the mall controversy. Then I asked Fran about the man in the limousine.

"Lots of rich people live in St. Andrews," Fran explained. "In the old days, they came from cities like Montreal to escape the humidity and relax in the summer breezes. They built some huge mansions."

"I've seen a few!"

"Of course, they had servants in those days. Butlers, maids, just like in the old movies. Some of them spent the entire summer in residence at the Algonquin Hotel, complete with butlers and maids. Even Sir John A. Macdonald stayed there."

"Speaking of movies," I whispered to Fran, "Colby Keaton is certain to become a star. See him talking to the guys at that fire truck? He's really something."

"He's an actor in your play?"

I nodded happily. Colby turned our way. I waved to him, just to be friendly. He waved back.

"When did the theater bug get to you, Liz?" Fran asked.

"Over in Charlottetown, I watched *Anne of Green Gables* from backstage. It was great! I auditioned for our school's musical last winter and got to be second lead. My mom thinks I might have enough talent to succeed."

Fran nodded. "So do I, which is why I suggested you to the director of *Annie*."

"I'm glad you did. I've always loved the story of Annie, an orphan, who meets a rich man from New York City. She's so charming with her singing and dancing that she wins him over and he wants to adopt her. But first he advertises everywhere to find her parents, and some crooks try to get the reward money he offers."

Fran nodded. "It's one of my favorite musicals, too."

"Hi," a voice sounded from behind.

I turned to see Colby standing behind me. Man, he was gorgeous. He had black wavy hair and beautiful blue eyes. We chatted about the fire for a few minutes, and then he turned to Fran. "How's business this summer?"

"Pretty good, thanks. My cabins are solidly booked for all of July, and August is looking good."

"If there was a mall, you'd be sold out summer and winter."

"I guess that's true," Fran said with a frown.

Colby smiled at me. "Feeling hungry, Liz? We could have a late-night snack at the Smuggler's Wharf."

"Sounds great." I looked at Fran. "Okay with you?"

She shook her head. "It's far too late."

"Okay," Colby said. "How about tomorrow night?"

When Fran gave her permission, I grinned with pleasure. What an added treat to an already exciting summer.

*   *   *

The next evening, I walked to the harbor with Colby. A pier extended out from shore; laughter and voices came across the water. The moon shone above.

Not far distant was the outline of Maine. The hillside twinkled with lights. I wondered if people would come across the border to see our show.

Time passed quickly with Colby. We had a window table, with a view of the moonlit boats in the harbor. We ate chowder and lobster rolls. The restaurant was decorated with hanging lamps and an ancient Union Jack flag. There was a waterwheel in the corner. It was a cosy place to be, and I felt good.

The outside door opened. "There's FDR," I said. "I think he's lonely."

We watched as FDR walked awkwardly across the restaurant to a table near us. His spectacles glittered in the lamplight. He gave his order to the waitress, waved at us, then opened a novel. I noticed that the cuffs of his trousers were frayed, and there were splits in the leather of his shoes.

"Heard the story on FDR?" Colby said, his voice low. "He lives by himself in an old house. His parents were

singers who entertained the wealthy visitors every summer at the hotel. When they retired, the hotel presented
them with an honorary key to the front door. Strange gift,
eh? Why not a gold Rolex? Anyway, when FDR's parents died, they left him a crumbly old house. People say
it's a strange place. It's full of his parents' mementoes,
photographs and stuff like that."

"What does he do?"

"Nothing. He lost his job as a teacher and can't get
another one."

"How is he able to live?"

"Probably on the last of the family bank account.
When that's gone, he's in deep trouble."

My hand brushed the salt cellar, which toppled over.
Fortunately, Colby was looking out the window, allow-
ing me to toss a pinch over my shoulder. I didn't know
what he might think of my superstitious nature.

Our young waitress, Bridget, arrived with more chowder for Colby. "You're from Winnipeg, right? Someone
said so. How do you like St. Andrews?" She asked.

"It's great! Full of excitement so far."

Bridget laughed. "For a small town, we have our
share. When the summer people aren't here to make it
lively, we have our own collection of eccentrics and
ghosts to keep the town talking. We even have our own
werewolf."

"Werewolf?" My heart started to pound as I remem-
bered the creature I saw the night before.

"It's just an old legend. Something the kids like to
scare themselves with," Bridget scoffed.

"They say a werewolf haunts Minister's Island," Colby
said, "but no one's ever seen it. I'll show you the island
someday."

"I think I saw something in the cemetery last night."

Bridget stared at me. "You actually saw the thing?"

"I don't know what I saw. Some kind of creature. I saw it just before the fire."

"Was it a werewolf?"

"I'm not . . ."

"Wow—I can't believe it's true!" Bridget raced to the kitchen, where we heard her going on about a werewolf in the Burying Ground. Then the door popped open, and the chef stared at me.

Colby smiled. "You're a star attraction tonight, Liz. Do you think what you saw was related to the fire?"

"I don't know. I'm not even sure of what I saw. I sure would like to get to the bottom of this."

"I heard you had a talent for sleuthing." Colby grinned and winked. "What a combo, beauty and brains."

I could feel my face turning a thousand shades of red. I turned away. I didn't particularly want Colby to see me do my neon light imitation.

Across the room, a couple was engaged in a heated debate. One wore a *Yes Mall* button, the other, a button that read *No Way*.

"I can see the mall is a hot topic here. How will the vote go, Colby? Any theories?"

"Funny you should ask," Colby said, producing some handwritten notes. "I've been following the debate and it's going to be close. At the beginning, it looked like the No's would take it. But, recently, several members have changed their minds. The Yes's are gaining support."

"What happens if it is a tie?"

"Then it is up to the chair, Mrs. O'Neal. If it's a tie, she casts the deciding vote. The fate of the mall could easily rest with her."

"I wouldn't want to be in her shoes."

On our table was an electric candle. It threw a soft light on Colby's face. "It's nice being with you, Liz. You've got that beautiful long hair and those ebony eyes."

"Thanks," I said, blushing. "Have you ever acted before, or is *Annie* your first time?"

"In high school I was in some plays, stuff like that." Colby put down his spoon. His blue eyes were thoughtful. "I really enjoy acting. You can be anything you want when you act." Colby looked at the sailboats riding at anchor on the dark water. "When I was a kid, I wanted to pitch in the majors. I'm a southpaw, and pretty good. But few players make it that far, so I quit. But acting is something I can do."

"How old are you, Colby?"

"I'm nineteen—been out of high school a couple of years. And you?"

"I'm sixteen, soon to be driving!" I grinned.

Bridget brought us dessert. "Rhubarb and strawberry pie," she said. "Our chef is famous for this."

Leaving the restaurant, we stopped at FDR's table. He was still reading his book, but he put it down to shake hands hello. "It's good to see you," he said.

"Likewise," I replied. "Colby says your parents were entertainers."

"That's correct," FDR beamed. The smile cheered up his face. "Come by my house some time, Liz, and I'll show you a few mementoes of their career."

"Thanks," I said. "I'd like that."

Outside the restaurant, Colby and I stood together in the warm night air, talking. I could smell the nearby sea. There were a few kids hanging around, and occasionally a car rolled slowly past. It was peaceful in St. Andrews, and the street looked pretty with its hanging flower baskets and old-fashioned streetlamps.

"My family owns a great old boat," Colby said. "It's a twenty-four-foot sloop-rigged Shark. Let's go sailing some time."

"Sounds great!"

He smiled. "How about tomorrow, before rehearsal."

"I can't. My friend Makiko arrives. She lives in Japan. Her father's company imports tuna from Prince Edward Island, where we met. Makiko and her father are in PEI again this summer, so she's coming here for a visit."

"Well, maybe some other time. I'll walk you home."

We saw few people as we walked through town. Then a black limousine came out of the night, moving slowly. A man leaned out the window, holding a leash. At its end, a poodle trotted beside the limo.

I laughed. "I saw that man at the fire. I guess he's walking the family dog."

"He's in the play, too. He plays Drake, the butler. Isn't that weird? In real life he's *got* a butler! Drake has a reputation for being a bit eccentric. Every year he likes to play a role in the local play."

"I saw him the other night. I'm looking forward to meeting him."

"Drake owns a lot of land around here," Colby said. "If the mall gets built, he'll be worth mega money. Real estate will be red hot. The mall's a great deal for this town. I think the Civic Trust should pass the bylaw."

"I don't envy the people on the Civic Trust," I said. "It'll be a tough decision to make."

Before I knew it, we had reached the Burying Ground. A shiver ran up my spine as I recalled the creature I saw.

"How about we check out that werewolf of yours?"

"I'm not sure it was a werewolf."

"There's only one way to find out."

I hesitated for a moment. I looked through the iron rails of the fence.

"Hey, Colby!" I grabbed his arm. "Something's in there!"

"Is it your creature?"

"I think so."

Within no time, we were under the trees, moving cautiously past the old graves. I checked the time on my watch. My nerves were strung tight. Ahead, we could see the figure kneeling on all fours at a grave, searching for something. Beside him was an old-fashioned lantern. A candle glowed inside it.

"Can you see what it is?" Colby whispered.

"I . . ."

At that moment, Colby stepped on a dead branch. The wood snapped loudly. The figure at the grave turned, looking our way. We both gasped aloud.

"Oh no," Colby exclaimed. "I don't believe my eyes!"

The figure's face seemed to be made of two different halves. On one side, its skin was bright red, thick and scarred. The features were distorted, almost completely gone. There was an eye, but no eyebrow, no hair on its head, not even an ear. The long dark hair on the other side of its head hung thick and tangled, like moss hanging from a tree.

The creature rose from its knees. Its eyes stared into the darkness, seeking us. As it turned to escape, one foot caught the lantern, knocking it over. The candle went out.

For a moment, I saw nothing. Then I detected the creature in the moonlight, fleeing across the cemetery.

"Come on, Colby," I yelled. We raced past the tombstones in pursuit.

"That's not a disguise," Colby cried as we ran. "That face is real. It's some kind of werewolf mutation."

In the shadow of the trees, I saw a white horse, tethered to the iron fence that surrounded the Burying Ground. The creature leapt to the top of the fence and, within moments, was galloping away into the night.

"The werewolf's escaping," Colby shouted. "We've got to capture it!"

We chased out of the Burying Ground, but the horse, with its rider, soon disappeared into the night.

"They're heading toward the sea," I said. "We'll never catch them."

Colby snapped his fingers. "I bet the werewolf has something to do with the fires."

"What makes you so sure?"

"Just a hunch."

"I'd like a bit more evidence before I come to any conclusions."

He shrugged. "You're the detective."

Colby escorted me home. The warm night air smelled deliciously of the sea. At my cabin we said goodnight. When Colby was gone, I walked across the lawn to the water. The moon was huge in the velvet night. Stars were scattered everywhere. I could see a satellite passing through space. I wondered where it came from, and what it meant.

Mostly, though, I wondered about the creature.

As I pondered, I heard the squeak of oars. In the path of moonlight, I saw a rowboat near the shoreline. FDR was at the oars, rowing intently. The moon glinted off his glasses and a few wisps of brown hair fell into his eyes.

I waved, and called hello, but FDR didn't seem to

notice. The rowboat just kept moving along the shore. I watched until it disappeared into the night.

"That's odd," I whispered to myself, and quickly returned to my cabin. Safely inside, I locked the door.

3

I didn't sleep well that night. Werewolf nightmares disturbed me. In the morning, I dragged myself outside. Birds twittered in the trees, as cheerful as the blue sky. I shook my head, trying to wake up.

The ocean was silver. I saw a sailboat running before the wind, and I wondered if Colby was out in his family's boat. Walking to the beach, I looked at the red sand. The wind had shaped it into ridges. Gulls perched on big rocks, taking the rays. "Makiko arrives today," I exclaimed to myself. "Finally, I get to see my friend again!"

At the Seaside Cabins office, I went inside. Fran was busy on the phone, but she waved. "Grab some orange juice."

In the kitchen, I sipped cold OJ while looking at the pictures on the fridge of Fran's nephews and nieces and the children of her friends. As I helped her prepare breakfast, I told her about Colby's view of the mall vote. We also talked about the creature. We were both still puzzled. "Maybe it's a mutation," I suggested. "Do they test nuclear fuel around here?"

"Not that I know of."

Outside in the morning sunlight, we walked along Water Street. People sat on their porches. They waved as we passed by. The houses were colorful and solid; they'd been built to last.

Only the occasional car was on the streets of the quiet town. A breeze touched the hanging flower baskets, and stirred the flags over shop doors. The town hall had two cannons in front, and the Shiretown Inn advertised that it had been in business since 1881. I knew Makiko would be taking lots of pictures.

"You know," Fran said, "St. Andrews must have looked exactly like this when the wealthy tourists first arrived. 'No hayfever and a railway' is how they advertised this town. It must have been nice at night, hearing the train's lonely whistle and the clackety-clack of the wheels."

She sighed. "St. Andrews is such a beautiful place— we'd be destroyed by a mall. I've been thinking about Colby's assessment of the members of the Civic Trust. He's right—the vote will be close. Greta O'Neal may indeed cast the decider."

"Was it always so close?"

"When the bylaw first became an issue, more members of the Civic Trust were against the mall. It seems in the last few weeks, somebody's been doing some pretty strong persuading."

"Why are they changing their minds?"

"Don't quote me on this, but two of the houses that burned belonged to people who were against the mall."

"But the third house is abandoned and doesn't belong to anybody."

Fran grinned. "It was just a theory. I didn't say it was a good one."

"If it's a tie, how will Mrs. O'Neal vote?"

Fran sighed. "I've been Greta O'Neal's friend for years. She's hugely proud of this town. She knows the risks of a mall, but she also knows jobs are important. It's a dilemma for her."

"Have you mentioned your feelings to her?" I asked.

"You bet. Me and everyone else in the town. She doesn't want to lose the way of life St. Andrews has to offer. But, then again, there are a lot of people in this town who need work, including Greta's son."

As we talked, we looked in shop windows, killing time while waiting for Makiko to arrive from the airport. I kept looking at my watch. "Makiko's parents know Mrs. O'Neal, so that's why she's staying there. But I already told you that, didn't I?"

Fran smiled. "Makiko and *Annie* are your favorite topics of conversation. By the way, I love your gift for Makiko."

"I bought the beaver and made the rest myself." I looked proudly at the furry little beaver in a Mountie uniform. He held the flags of Canada and Japan.

"How long until Makiko joins her Dad in PEI?"

"Two weeks is all we've got," I said sadly. "But it'll be a great time, and she'll be in the audience when our musical opens."

"Let's head for Greta O'Neal's house," Fran said. "They'll be arriving soon."

We hurried through the leafy streets. The green yards were shaded and looked cool in the brightness of the morning sun. A man swung in a hammock, listening to a baseball game on the radio. Kids smiled at us as they rode past on bikes. Everyone was taking it easy. It was a quiet, peaceful town.

Ahead, I could see Mrs. O'Neal's house. It was brick with three chimneys and a carved arch over the door. Fran told me that it was built well over a hundred years ago.

I saw a car coming in our direction. Makiko was in the passenger seat, grinning at me. She waved, and I waved. The car stopped, and Makiko jumped out. I started running, so did she, and then we were hugging each other in the middle of the street. It was really great to see her again. Her eyes were shining, and her black hair glowed in the sunlight.

We babbled away, covering a dozen different subjects as we walked to the house, arm in arm. Makiko gave me a Japanese fan decorated with delicate flowers in gold and red, and I presented the little beaver. Fran and Mrs. O'Neal watched our exchange of gifts. Mrs. O'Neal, whose neatly trimmed grey hair and elegant suit gave her a business-like air, beamed with pleasure.

"Well!" She smiled. "You girls are so thrilled to see each other! It does my heart good."

We all went inside. "Let me show you around," Mrs. O'Neal said. "This house was built early in the nineteenth century. Back then it was called Chestnut Hall."

The house was filled with antiques. Mahogany, polished oak, crystal, grandfather clocks, silver cutlery, everything.

"You've got the whole nine yards," I exclaimed to Mrs. O'Neal. "This place is a museum! People must have had a great life back then."

"Actually," she said, "people lived mostly in the dark and cold. Just imagine—they wore the same things all winter, day and night. They *slept* in their clothes."

Makiko's black eyes grew larger. "Is that true?"

Mrs. O'Neal nodded. "Oh yes. They were trying not to catch a cold, because people died easily. They didn't have the benefit of our modern medicines." She shook her head. "The women wore enormous hairdos that they rarely took down or washed. I don't know how they slept."

Mrs. O'Neal led us up a curved staircase. "This was designed for protection against attack in the night. A robber was forced to use his gun-hand to follow the curving handrail."

"Ah!" Makiko's eyes lit up. "The robber cannot also hold his gun. The owner gains extra moments for defence."

"Exactly."

Mrs. O'Neal gave us a tour of the upper floor. We saw more antiques, as well as her personal office, which was equipped with all the modern technology. My favorite room was Makiko's, with its four-poster bed. The bed was so high off the ground that steps were needed to climb into it.

Mrs. O'Neal took a pair of white satin wedding shoes from a cupboard. "These have been passed down for generations. Notice the mark of the Paris shoemaker? I show these to all my guests."

*   *   *

With the tour over, Mrs. O'Neal led us back downstairs.

"Who's for a snack?" she asked, rubbing her stomach. "I've made some pound cake. The recipe's from a cookbook published over a century and a half ago. The cake uses nine eggs and a pound of butter. Nobody knew about cholesterol in 1839!"

The pound cake was fabulous. We sat in the kitchen, surrounded by the past, stuffing our faces and talking to Mrs. O'Neal about the town. She'd lived here her whole life—sixty-five years.

"You'll like St. Andrews," she said to us, "there's lots to do. My daughter's two mountain bikes are outside in the garage. You're welcome to use them. She moved away last year, to Boston. She teaches at one of the universities there."

"Look," I said, pointing out the window. We all looked out at the street where a small girl was zooming in circles on a pink bike. "That's Emily. She was at the fire the other night, with her mother."

"They're my new neighbors," Mrs. O'Neal said. "I don't know much about them. The mother seems very nice. The stepfather keeps to himself."

"Who owned the empty house that was torched the other night?" I asked.

Mrs. O'Neal hesitated. "The town, but I was going to buy it. The town had accepted my offer. We were just drawing up the papers."

Fran and I exchanged a worried look. It seemed that Fran's theory might be correct. The arson *was* related to the vote.

"Would that property be worth more if the mall gets built?" I asked.

"I suppose it would," Mrs. O'Neal replied. "But the land with real potential is north of town, where the mall would be. Imagine the value of that real estate."

"Any idea why the arson happened, Mrs. O'Neal?"

She shook her head. "Not unless it's connected somehow to my vote on the mall. But . . ."

Just then a phone beeped at her side. Mrs. O'Neal picked it up. As she listened to the caller, her face slowly went white. Her hand rose to her throat. Hanging up the phone, she stared at us.

"I've just been threatened."

"What happened?" we all exclaimed.

She stared at the phone. "It was some man. His voice was disguised. He said, 'Support the mall or the werewolf strikes again.' Those were his exact words."

Fran picked up the phone. "I'm calling the cops."

"I'm so frightened of fire," Mrs. O'Neal said. "I've been receiving calls for the last few days, but usually the caller doesn't say anything, and just hangs up. This is the first time I've been threatened."

Fran patted her hand. "Please, Greta, don't let it rattle you. And don't let it affect your vote."

Mrs. O'Neal's teacup trembled as she raised it. "I won't, don't worry. I plan to make up my own mind, although I'm torn how to choose."

"You know what the mall will mean to the future of our town," Fran said quietly.

"You know as well as I, Fran, how much I love St. Andrews and its way of life," Mrs. O'Neal replied, "but what future do we have if everyone leaves because there is no work?"

"Who's against building the mall?" I asked.

"A lot of people oppose it, including most of the summer people. They own exquisite old houses and have lots of money. They live here during the good weather, and they want things peaceful."

"A mall could change all that," I said. "This town is

so beautiful, Mrs. O'Neal. Every house is a postcard scene. It would be ruined!"

"I agree with you and must consider the interests of the people who oppose the mall. But what about the jobs? I have to consider that, too."

I shook my head. "I don't know. It just seems sad." Through the window, I watched Emily playing on her bike. "Think about the kids, Mrs. O'Neal. Maybe they want a peaceful town when they're older. You should ask them! It's their future you're deciding."

"You're right. They are another group whose interests I should consider." Mrs. O'Neal sighed. "It's all so very complicated."

The back door opened. In came Mrs. O'Neal's son and his wife, and three little kids. They swarmed around their grandmother, collecting kisses and cookies, then the family presented Makiko with sweet-smelling flowers for her room.

Mrs. O'Neal's son sent the kids outside. He looked at his mother. "I think we've made a decision."

Her eyes filled with tears. "I've been dreading this. You're leaving town, aren't you?"

He nodded. "Please don't cry, Mom. There's no work here."

"Where are you going?" Mrs. O'Neal asked.

"Out west. I heard about a job in Lethbridge, Alberta."

"That's so far away."

Fran signalled to us, and we slipped out the door. "Let's leave them be," Fran said. Her voice was tight with emotion.

Makiko wiped away a tear. "My heart is sad."

We walked through town, talking about Mrs. O'Neal's dilemma. After saying goodbye to Fran, I headed for the theater with Makiko. "I can't wait to show you the Burying Ground," I said, "and tell you what happened. It was creepy for sure." I looked at my watch. "After rehearsal, we can check the graveyard for clues."

Makiko smiled. "Our first adventure began in a cemetery, on beloved Prince Edward Island."

*   *   *

The theater where we were rehearsing *Annie* was on a tree-shaded street. Inside, we walked down the aisle past rows of empty seats. Makiko was nervous about being introduced.

There was all kinds of action on stage. Colby was talking to Drake, the Rockettes were warming up at the *barre,* and the orphans were singing "Tomorrow" led by Margaret, the music director.

Finished with their song, the orphans swarmed around Makiko as I performed introductions. Emily held back, so I brought Makiko over to her. Emily's enormous brown eyes gazed at Makiko as she managed a small hello. One of the other orphans turned to me. Her name was Ashlee. "Is it true you actually *saw* the St. Andrews werewolf? Everyone says so."

All their eyes stared at me.

"Well," I said, "I don't know if it was a werewolf, but I saw something unusual, that's for sure."

"Then it's true!" Ashlee stared at the other orphans. "The werewolf is for real!"

"Hold on," I said, "I didn't say there was a werewolf."

But it was useless. The girls chattered excitedly to each other. "We know where the werewolf comes from," a girl named Tegan said to me. "It haunts the old mansion, over on Minister's Island."

"That's right," another orphan exclaimed. "Long ago, the island was owned by Sir William Van Horne, the guy who built the Canadian Pacific Railway across Canada. It was his summer place—he came down from Montreal in his private railway car and lived there. He built a man-sion—it's huge. They had lots of parties, then Sir William died. Now a weird woman and her servant live over there. Nobody's allowed on the island. If you go over, you'll get chased with an axe."

"Not an axe," Tegan said. "A shotgun."

"Why do you think the mansion is haunted?" I asked.

"There's all kinds of stories," Ashlee replied. "Some kids snuck onto the island last year. It was night-time. They saw something *creepy* run through the moonlight. It had a weird face and long hair—it looked like fur, they said. They were lucky to get away alive! Nobody's been back since."

"So," another girl added, "don't you get it? The were-wolf haunts the island. That's what those kids saw in the moonlight. It was the werewolf! Now it's come over to town, to get *us*."

As the orphans buzzed with excitement, we were joined by Colin Skinner, the director of *Annie*. He had lots of curly hair and a nice smile. Colin was really tal-ented and nice. He made everyone feel at ease. In the first act, I'd be a hobo living under a bridge, then later a chorus dancer with the Rockettes, and then a singer on a New York street.

I introduced Makiko to Colin and then to Nicholas and Barbara, a brother and sister team of singers. Then FDR rolled over in the old-fashioned wheelchair he used in the play; it was just like the wooden wheelchair once used by the real-life president.

Drake was there. He wore a gold watch chain and a black coat with dress-tails hanging down. I thought he looked like a real snob. "Do you disapprove of how I walk my poodle? You and Colby seemed quite amused last night."

I shrugged my shoulders. "Using a limousine to walk your dog isn't good for the environment. It pollutes the air."

Drake sniffed loudly, gave me a beady-eyed look, then walked away. A couple of girls smiled and gave me a thumb's up.

I noticed Emily looking at me from one of the old-fashioned dormitory beds used in the show. Her eyes seemed to call me.

I walked over. "Okay to join you? I saw you riding your bike earlier." I sat on the bed. The frame was made of iron and the creak of the springs bothered my teeth. "How old are you, Emily?"

"Nine."

"Wow—I'm impressed you're on the stage already."

She looked toward the other orphans. "The youngest one," she whispered, "is only seven, and *totally* talented."

"Aren't you friends with them?"

She shrugged. "I like to be alone."

Emily was wearing a sweatshirt over unitards with leg warmers and jazz shoes. She looked well-groomed, except for her fingernails. They were grubby and bitten down.

Seeing my stare, Emily hastily closed her hands. "That was brave, Liz, the way you saved the kitty from the fire. I'm not brave at all."

"What are you talking about? You're brave enough to go on stage. What's it like playing an orphan?"

"Kind of fun." For the first time, her brown eyes looked happy. "Acting's good for me," she whispered.

"At home, I stay in my room with the door locked, and I act out stories."

"Why do you lock the door?"

Emily stared at me. Something happened inside her eyes. She looked frightened.

Then Colin Skinner called for attention. "Let's get to work. Orphans and Drake, I'll need you, please."

Like a summer storm, Emily's fear quickly passed away. She got up and stood at the front of the stage with the rest of the orphans.

Emily was loaded with talent. Besides being an orphan, she'd been chosen Annie's understudy. That meant Emily would take over the main role if Annie got sick or was unable to perform. Emily had to rehearse the part so she knew it perfectly.

"Okay, Emily," Colin said, "let's try Annie's first number."

Emily nodded and took her place on the stage. When Emily sang her song, she was exuberant, bubbling with energy and charm.

I stood beside FDR, watching her rehearse. "Emily is transformed into another person on stage," FDR said. "I guess she's happiest as an entertainer. My parents were the same."

"They must have had an interesting life."

"They did. You've seen the tower at the hotel? The room at the top is called the Eagle's Nest. It's reached by circular stairs. My parents were singers in the Nest. Once a week, I sit there drinking a Perrier, looking at the lights below, watching the moonlight on the sea, reliving my parents' glory days." He sighed. "The Eagle's Nest remains exactly how they left it. The same piano, the same furniture. It's a shrine, I guess."

*   *   *

After rehearsal I stayed on stage, talking to Colby. He wanted me to go sailing, but I'd planned to spend time with Makiko.

"Makiko's anxious to explore the Burying Ground, so we're going together."

"Too bad," Colby said. "I brought my camera to get some pictures of you, out on the ocean."

Something fluttered in my stomach whenever he smiled. I admit it—I was disappointed. "I promised Makiko," I said. "But maybe another time."

As I packed up my gear to leave the theater, I saw Emily in the orphans' dressing room. She sat on a bench, looking at me. At her feet was a bouquet of wilted wild-flowers. The other orphans had left things in a jumble, but Emily's rehearsal outfit and shoes were neatly put away.

"Why haven't you gone home, Emily?" I asked, going into the room.

Her huge eyes watched me. On her forehead were tiny droplets of sweat. "My stomach hurts."

"I'm sorry," I said, taking her hand. "How can I help?"

"Maybe walk me home?"

"Sure thing."

Outside the theater, Makiko was talking to Miss Hanni-gan. In the play, she's a tyrant who rules the orphanage with an iron fist, but offstage she was very nice. Miss Hannigan was a local teacher. In real life, her name was Mrs. Smith. She had a super-nice husband and two adorable little kids.

"I'm in a show every summer," Miss Hannigan told Makiko. "I've loved acting since I was very young."

I walked up Prince of Wales Drive with Makiko and Emily. The street was thick with trees; the thousands of leaves were green in the sunshine. Outside one of the pretty houses, a man pushed a mower across a big yard while a woman took in laundry and a child played in a sandbox.

"It's a beautiful town, Emily. Do you like it here?"

She didn't reply. Ahead of us was the blackened shell of the house torched the night before last. It smelled of fire. "Feel like investigating?" I asked Makiko.

She grinned and nodded. "The game's afoot, in words of most admired Sherlock Holmes."

We searched around the house, looking for signs of the van I had seen the night of the fire.

"Darn," I said, studying the hard-packed ground beside the road. "No chance of tire tracks."

Makiko picked up a tiny chunk of dried mud. "This is red, like island home of beloved Anne. Earth here is brown. Perhaps mud fell from van."

Emily said, "There are fields with red soil outside town. There's a carnival playing there."

"Excellent information," I said. "Thanks, Emily!"

A grin split her face, then she became solemn again. "You're welcome, Liz."

I looked at Makiko. "We should go to see that carnival together. Maybe we can learn something. Carnivals play all over Canada, every summer. They're bizarre."

"I would love to go, Liz," my friend replied. "But first, let us see the Burying Ground."

The Burying Ground looked scary, even in daylight. Makiko's eyes were solemn as she studied the enormously tall trees shading the old tombstones. The iron fence was like a row of spears, spikes up.

The iron gate squealed rustily as we entered the cemetery. I watched a leaf tumble down and caught it. "That's for luck," I said. "A falling leaf is a nice talisman." I swallowed, and looked around the gloomy cemetery.

"But it's no guarantee."

We found the grave where I'd seen the creature. "Look," Makiko said, examining the ground. "Knees of some person have pressed into soft soil."

"You're right, and here's the lantern. It got kicked under this shrub." I held it up. The glass was that old-fashioned bumpy kind, and the iron was heavy. "There's a name stamped in the iron. *Coven Hoven.*" I picked up some roses from the grave. "The creature may have left these, too."

"Coven Hoven is the name of the mansion on Minister's Island!" Emily exclaimed.

"Thanks, Emily, that really helps." I smiled at her. But inside, I shivered. Maybe what the orphans said about the werewolf on the island was correct.

We left the lantern in the cemetery, in case the creature came looking for it. The thought of it looking through the town for its lantern gave me the shivers.

I have to admit, I felt a lot better once we had left the dusky cemetery and stood in the brightness of the streets. The change had an effect on Emily, too, for suddenly she burst out, "Would you come riding with me sometime? Please, Liz. Please, Makiko. I've got a horse. His name is Midnight. You'll love him."

I stared at Emily, amazed at the sudden torrent of words. Then I smiled. "Sure, Emily, that's a great idea."

"Thank you!" She looked at her watch and grew solemn again. "I'm really late home. I can't stay any longer. I wish I could."

"Shall I walk you the rest of the way?"

"No thanks, Liz. I'll be okay."

With great reluctance, Emily trudged away. Makiko watched her go. "Such a melancholy child," she said. "My heart is deeply touched."

4

"Do you think the creature is setting fires, Liz?" Makiko asked as we walked through town.

"I don't know. But I think whoever or whatever started the fire got away in that van I saw."

At the edge of town, we ran into Colby. "How's the sleuthing business?" he asked. I told him about the lantern we'd found. Then Makiko explained our theory about the mud being linked to the carnival outside town. "We're going there now," I said, "to check for a van. Maybe this mud fell from the one I saw the other night."

"The carnival doesn't open until dusk," Colby said. "Want to go sailing until then?"

Makiko's eyes lit up. "Oh, yes. Yes, please, Keaton-san."

"Keaton-san? What's that mean?"

I smiled. "It's the Japanese way of honoring a person they've met, Colby. Makiko used to call me Austen-san."

On our way through town, Colby stopped to buy a picnic basket filled with goodies. "Maybe we'll get marooned on a desert island," he smiled. "We'll need provisions."

We walked out along the long wooden pier together. It was busy. Makiko took so many pictures her camera was practically smoking. But I had to admit that it was a lovely scene with the white sailboats at anchor and the gulls floating among sparkling diamonds of sunlight.

We bought ice cream from a little refreshment booth and discussed the other tourists as we ate. Then, while Colby made a call from a pay phone, Makiko and I talked to a couple of university students who'd cycled all the way from Québec. They were really sunburned, but cheerful.

"What is that?" one asked, pointing at a huge building on a hill, high above St. Andrews.

"That's the Algonquin Hotel," I replied. "Impressive, eh? In the old days, wealthy people came to the Algonquin with butlers and maids."

"The original hotel caught fire one day in 1914," Colby said, joining us. "There was a wind, so it burned like a torch. The flames must have been spectacular. I wish I could have seen it."

Soon, the sailboat was running before the wind. I wasn't nervous—Colby was a good sailor. We skimmed along the shoreline, splattered by flecks of spray from the bow.

"There's Fran!"

She was out in a kayak, not far from her cabins.

"Fran," I yelled. "This is the life!"

She called back, but I couldn't hear. I waved, then smiled at Colby. Holding the tiller, I felt the strength of the wind in the sail. "The sea's so vast," I said to Makiko. She was studying the shoreline through miniaturized binoculars. "We could sail together to foreign shores, discovering the world."

Makiko nodded, lowering her binoculars. "We are kindred spirits, Liz."

Colby pointed toward shore. "That's where the mall's going to be built," he said. "The land's worth a fortune, if the vote goes through."

"Somebody is willing to do anything to make sure it's a yes vote. Even destroy property," I said.

"What's your theory, Liz?"

"Several Civic Trust members have changed their votes to yes since the arson began. Now some flea-brain is pressuring Mrs. O'Neal because it looks as if the vote will be a tie. They're threatening to burn her house if she doesn't vote for the mall."

Colby looked at me. "What do you mean?"

"It's a stupid strategy, Colby. It's horrible and destructive. Mrs. O'Neal seems like a courageous woman. Threats won't make her back down." I studied the shoreline through Makiko's binoculars. "Does Drake own all that land?"

"Who knows?" Colby replied. "I've heard different stories."

"We'd better check it out, Makiko. The town archives might have some information."

"Detectives at work," Colby grinned. "I love it." He put his arm around me, and Makiko took another picture of us. The wind swept through my hair, and the sun warmed my face. The ocean was beautiful. Waves leapt around us, almost as if they were dancing. After a while, Colby trained his binoculars on an island. It was very large and green and appeared empty except for a big house standing alone above the sea. A shiver passed through me, as though somehow I'd been drawn by destiny to this place.

"You're looking at Minister's Island," Colby said. "That mansion is Coven Hoven."

Makiko nodded. "Famous home of famous man, Sir William Van Horne of the Canadian Pacific Railway. In school, I have studied his story."

"Van Horne was quite a character. He bought that entire island. It's huge. You could spend hours exploring, if you were allowed. Van Horne had the servants cut a pool into the rocks. Every day it filled with sea water, and he went swimming. He didn't build a house, he built a mansion. It's got eleven bathrooms!"

"Why won't the new owners allow anyone on the island?" I asked.

Colby shrugged. "Who knows? Hey, have you heard about the Road Beneath the Sea?"

We shook our heads.

"Minister's Island is connected to the mainland by a neck of land. At low tide it's exposed, so people can reach the island. Not that anyone is welcome there. At high tide, covered by water, it becomes the Road Beneath the Sea."

I looked at Makiko. "That road could be dangerous."

"In Van Horne's day, some people got trapped out there in a horse-and-buggy," Colby said. "The tide came on too fast for them to reach land. The horse got spooked. It froze in fear as the water rose. One person left the buggy and made it to shore, but two others drowned."

Colby dropped anchor, and we were floating on the water, far from shore. We sat on deck, eating the picnic and watching the patterns change on the water. It was so peaceful that we stayed until after the yellow sun had burned down into the sea.

The moment it was gone, the air grew cold. We put on extra gear and listened to the birds call across the darkening water. A few clouds drifted above us. For a long time no one spoke. Then Colby said, "Feel like exploring Minister's Island?"

"Will we cross the Road Beneath the Sea?" I asked. "The sailboat might run aground."

Colby shook his head. "The road's on the other side of the island."

I looked at Minister's Island. Steep bluffs rose above us. Trees were silhouetted against the dark sky. No lights were visible. I looked at Makiko. "If we can prove there's no werewolf here, we might be closer to solving the mystery. Want to check it out? We could go to the carnival tomorrow evening."

She studied the grim island, then swallowed bravely. "Yes," she said. "Let us be brave."

"We'll lower the sail and row ashore near Van Horne's bathhouse," Colby said. "It's a tower in the cliffside, with stairs inside. That's how Van Horne reached his luxurious seawater swimming pool. Man, that guy could live."

*   *   *

The bathhouse was creepy inside. Every sound echoed as we climbed the stairs. I tried not to touch the cold walls. Makiko's black eyes were enormous. "*Ganbatte,*" she whispered in Japanese. "We must press on."

At the top of the cliff, the light of the moon was cold, shining down on Coven Hoven. The mansion was an ominous sight, dark and silent. I saw power lines strung along sagging poles, but not a light was visible. A wind swept around the mansion and stirred the trees, making a rustling noise.

"I keep feeling like someone's watching us," I said.

"Want to leave?" Colby asked.

In the moonlight, he was so good-looking. No way was I wimping out. "Let's explore," I said. "That's why we're here."

Something screeched in the woods.

I gulped. "An owl . . . I think."

Staying together, we moved along a path. The lawn was a jungle, and the flower beds had no flowers. I looked at the woods, where the moonlight slanted down. Something ran through the shadows.

I grabbed Makiko's arm. "Did you see that?"

She nodded.

I pointed into the woods. "Look!"

Visible among the trees was a face, almost hidden behind tangled, thick hair. Around one of the eyes, the skin was shiny red and puckered. The lips were twisted open.

Then, suddenly, the face was gone.

"It's the creature," I whispered, my voice disappearing with fear.

Colby's voice trembled. "It's true! There *is* a werewolf!" He looked at us. "We'd better get moving."

"You're right," I said, and Makiko nodded.

We ran as quickly as we could to the boat.

When we reached the bathhouse, I stopped and looked back at the dark shape of Coven Hoven, still certain we were being watched. What was the mansion's secret? I wanted to know more.

5

In the morning, I did some research. Most communities save old books, newspapers and other information as part of their history; in St. Andrews, these archives are stored at the Old Gaol.

Conditions were rough for prisoners back when the Old Gaol was a jail. I studied a couple of the cells, picturing people crowded together inside the thick walls, miserable and cold. Then, shivering, I headed for one of the cosy research rooms.

Digging around in the archive files, I found some notes written in the southpaw slant of a left-handed writer. The notes were about local land ownership. I started to read about the ownership history of the potentially valuable property north of town. Part of the land was held for a long time by a family named Dodge.

"That's FDR's family," I said aloud.

I turned the page, hoping to discover more, but the page I wanted was missing.

Curious, I decided to try some cross-referencing with back issues of the local newspaper on microfiche. After a lot of looking, I found the article I wanted. I looked at a photograph of Drake, the butler in our play. He was much younger then, with more hair. He had just bought the land at the north end of town. The deal gave him total control of the area. He'd purchased the land from the estate of FDR's parents. An editorial in the same issue questioned the whole deal. The writer of the piece didn't like the way the transaction was handled. The article made some interesting points, so I jotted down a few of them in my notebook.

Later on, I checked the index for Minister's Island— there was a lot to study. I read about the days of Van Horne, how his servants strung nets in the orchard so the peaches wouldn't bruise falling from the trees, and how he built a huge barn to raise expensive cattle. Van Horne was a painter. He also liked to pamper his grandson with every kind of toy. He accomplished all this, *and* he built a railroad that spanned Canada from sea to sea.

After Van Horne's death, the island passed through several owners until it was purchased by Lady Chandler and her husband. There was another article that caught my eye. I made some hasty notes. Finding nothing else of interest, I took what I had written and hurried through town to Mrs. O'Neal's house.

*   *   *

I was anxious to discuss my findings with Makiko. She was in the kitchen, sipping tea with Mrs. O'Neal and Fran. On the table, Makiko had some articles about overdevelopment and the bad effects it has on a town.

Mrs. O'Neal smiled. "Have you come to convince me to vote no, too, Liz?"

"I think Makiko and Fran are probably doing a good enough job," I replied.

"We're talking about a way of life, Greta," Fran said. "A way you believe in, a way you'll lose."

"I know," Mrs. O'Neal sighed.

"It would be unfortunate if St. Andrews became polluted. It has happened in my country." Makiko added, "It is a very sad thing."

"There are good arguments for the mall," Mrs. O'Neal replied, "and good arguments against it."

I asked if she'd talked to any kids.

Mrs. O'Neal looked down at her teacup. "No, I haven't."

Fran leaned toward her. "Give it a try, Greta. You're deciding their future."

"Everybody's future is at stake," Mrs. O'Neal replied quietly. "But will we have a future if there are no jobs?"

Fran reached across the table and took Mrs. O'Neal's hand in hers. She squeezed it gently. "I think I've pressured you enough for one day. Do you have any of that pound cake left?"

As we ate our cake, I told the others what I'd learned about Coven Hoven. "There must be a good reason for all the secrecy," Fran said. "There's a servant who comes into town for supplies and he's not friendly at all."

I left the house with Makiko. As we walked toward the theater, I told her about my discoveries at the archives.

"Fifteen years ago, a man and woman died on Minister's Island in a car crash. September 9th was the date of the crash."

"Why is date important?" Makiko asked.

"At the Burying Ground, the creature was kneeling at a grave. It had two names on it, but only a single date for when they died. That means they died together. On the tombstone was a year, followed by 9-9. I remember it."

"9-9?"

"That means the ninth day of the ninth month. That couple died on Minister's Island on September 9th, fifteen years ago. That same date was on the grave."

"Very interesting, Liz, but what does it mean?"

"I'm not sure, but it may have something to do with all of the secrecy at Coven Hoven."

Then I told her all I had discovered about the land on the north end of town.

"So, FDR may have a claim to the land for mall," Makiko concluded after hearing all the facts.

"If he can prove that Drake acquired the land illegally from his parents' estate."

"Why doesn't he do so now?"

"I don't know. Maybe he's waiting until the mall is built. The land would be worth lots more then."

"Maybe FDR-san not know he may have claim," Makiko suggested.

"Could be. It all happened a long time ago."

*   *   *

Makiko and I entered the theater. I went on stage and she sat in the audience. Some dancers were warming up, Colby was rehearsing one of his numbers and the orphans were braiding each other's hair as they waited their turn.

Emily sat apart from them.

Her eyes looked tired as I dropped down on the floor to say hello.

"How are you?" I asked.

"Fine!" She pasted on a smile. "How are you, Liz?"

Wondering if she was lonely, I got a brainwave. "Emily, I've got a surprise for you."

"What is it?"

"Tell you later." I smiled at her. "It'll be fun."

Colby came over and joined me. My heart fluttered a little as he sat down beside me. I got a whiff of his cologne. It had a nice, clean scent.

"Being on the island was nervous work," he said. "That thing in the woods scared me!"

Ashlee, who was walking by, stopped and stared at him, then me. "You saw something on the island? Was it the werewolf?"

"I don't know," I replied. "But . . ."

Before I could continue, I was surrounded by a pack of orphans, every one of them eager to discuss the werewolf. All of them had a lot of information about werewolves that they were eager to share. Each of them seemed to enjoy scaring the rest of the group with what they knew.

"Werewolves come out only when there's a full moon."

"Some werewolves are werewolves all the time."

"That's not true," Colby said, lowering his voice. The orphans became silent, waiting to hear what he might say next. "When people are turned into werewolves, they become vicious beasts. They can't control themselves and are capable of any kind of destruction. But, during the day, when they are not werewolves, they look like ordinary, nice people. In fact, usually the quietest, meekest person by day is a werewolf by night."

The girls screamed and laughed, delighted to be so frightened.

"I know who the werewolf is, then," Ashlee said solemnly. "He's here in the theater." Her eyes darted across the stage to Colin, who was talking to Drake, Miss Hannigan and FDR.

"Who?" the orphans all asked at once, anxious to know.

"It's FDR. He's quiet and meek." Several orphans nodded in agreement.

"That's not proof," I argued.

"There's something else," Tegan said. "Werewolves are afraid of dogs." She pointed at Sandy the collie who had a "walk-on" role in our musical. "She's the world's friendliest collie, but FDR is really scared of her."

"Lots of people are scared of dogs."

Ashlee touched my arm. "FDR is one of the undead. He carries the curse of the werewolf."

"How do you know that?"

"He's weird—he lives alone."

"So does Fran. She's not a werewolf."

"Hey," Molly exclaimed, "maybe she is!"

"Oh, good grief." I slapped my forehead. "Fran is not a werewolf, and neither is FDR."

"But, FDR's always going over to Minister's Island and nobody knows why. So, that proves it," Ashlee said, with a nod of her head.

I didn't believe that FDR was the werewolf, but that didn't mean he wasn't linked to the arson. Later, when the orphans were rehearsing, I told Colby all I had learned about FDR and the land slated for the mall.

"FDR could make a lot of money if the mall were built and he claimed the land," Colby concluded. "And FDR sure needs money."

"Drake could make money, too. Maybe he's behind the arson."

Colby's face twitched. "That's too obvious. I think it's FDR. He looks like a nice guy on the surface, but you never know what's going on underneath. Kind of like a werewolf."

It wasn't a nice thought. But I had other things I wanted to discuss.

"Colby, I've got an idea. Emily seems sad today, so I thought a surprise might cheer her up. But I need your help."

I whispered my plan, and he liked the idea. We made arrangements. Then we chatted with Judge Brandeis and FDR, who rolled over in his wooden chair.

"One of the boys was popping wheelies in this chair," FDR grinned. "But I'm no good at it." He gave me a slip of paper. "Please come for a visit tonight. Here's my address. Bring your pal, Makiko. You can see my parents' mementoes. Later this summer, we'll visit the Eagle's Nest, where they performed. The hotel's closed now for renovations, but we'll see the Nest before you leave town. It's part of local history."

"That's a nice invitation," I said, smiling.

The moment rehearsal ended, Emily hurried to me. Her eyes were shining. "What's the surprise, Liz? Is it an adventure?"

"You'll know soon, Emily."

Feeling delighted with my brainwave, I finalized the secret arrangements with Colby. Then Emily and I found Makiko in the lobby, and we went outside into the warm sunshine.

As we walked through town, Makiko praised Emily's singing and she beamed with pleasure. "I think Colby's in love with Liz. Right, Makiko?"

Makiko's eyes sparkled. "Emily-san has strong powers of observation."

I blushed. "Give me a break, guys."

"He's cute," Emily said.

Laughing, I gave Emily a hug. It was good to see her so happy.

But then it ended.

The moment we reached the pier I felt Emily tense up. "Why are we here, Liz? I don't want ice cream."

"We didn't come for cones, Emily. This is your surprise."

Her dark eyes stared at me. Already big, they grew bigger. "Here?"

"Yes! Colby went ahead—he's waiting for us."

As we walked along the pier, Makiko took pictures. I had to force my smiles for the camera because Emily was suddenly so anxious. Her eyes darted back to Water Street. She was taking deep breaths.

Colby waited in his sailboat beside a lower dock. A long, steep ramp led to it. Emily took one step down, then froze.

"I can't," she whispered.

"It's okay, Emily," I said. "I've got another idea. How about if I meet your horse?"

She nodded her head vigorously.

I looked at Colby. Sunshine touched his hair. "We'll try another time. Okay with you?"

"Sure!" Colby winked at Makiko. "How about you, Makiko-san? Care for a sail?"

"Gracious thanks," she replied, "but, please, may I accept a check of the rain?"

He grinned. "I think you mean a rain check, Makiko. You've got it, for sure."

So, in the end, Colby sailed alone. As we walked along

the pier, we saw his Shark leave the harbor. The sail dipped low, caught by the wind as it headed for the open seas.

Makiko decided to spend the afternoon at home. "I shall correspond with my family. Many postcards remain to be sent. A pleasant time awaits me. Perhaps O'Neal-san will offer tea with chocolate pound cake as I write my cards."

"What'll you tell your family about St. Andrews?" Emily asked.

"It is paradise."

I grinned. "Tell them for me, too." I turned to Emily. "I bet I can guess the color of your horse. It's black."

"Wow! I'm impressed."

"It wasn't difficult," I admitted. "After all, you named him Midnight."

"Sorry you missed your sailboat ride, Liz."

"I don't mind, Emily. But I'm curious. What bothered you?"

"Well . . ." She took a deep breath. "Well, it's the ocean." Her eyes stared down. "I . . . I'm scared of water."

"That's okay, Emily," I said. "I'm scared of heights. That's why I go on rides at carnivals—I won't give in to the fear."

"Does it work?"

"There'll always be some goosebumps. But fear doesn't keep me from having fun."

Makiko took our picture together. "Emily-san," she said gently, "each person has strength. It is waiting inside you, like a treasure. When you find your courage, it never leaves again. It will give you peace."

I confess I was lost, but Emily wasn't. She stared at Makiko. "Yes," she said. "I understand."

*   *   *

We dropped Makiko off at Mrs. O'Neal's and continued to a barn outside town. Inside, Emily fed Midnight a carrot and he rubbed his face against her shoulder. She busied herself brushing his coat. "Be careful," she warned, when I came close. "Midnight is head shy."

I like horses but not when they bite, so I kept clear of Midnight's stall. Wandering around the barn, I breathed the rich smells of hay and oats. I ran my hand over a bridle's chain, which tinkled softly, and listened to the pleasant sounds of the horses munching their food.

Emily's mother came into the barn. She asked if I was enjoying St. Andrews, then smiled tenderly at her daughter. She looked at her watch. "This is my day off work and I'd hoped to ride, but it's later than I thought. Liz, would you care to take my horse, Lightning, today? I'm sure Emily would enjoy your company."

When I said yes, Emily's eyes lit up.

"It's nice to see Emily smile," her mother said. Her eyes were solemn as she stroked Emily's hair. "She's always been a quiet child."

Soon I was up in the saddle, sniffing the air as Lightning and Midnight walked placidly along a pleasant wooded trail. Lightning blew softly through her nose as I patted her warm neck and listened to her tail switching away flies.

"You're a good rider," I told Emily.

"I love to ride."

"So do I. Which do you like better, acting or riding?"

Emily scrunched up her eyes and thought a moment. "I like both the best, but maybe I like acting more."

I laughed. "Me too. The more we rehearse, the more I enjoy it. I think I'm hooked."

Emily was silent for a while. Then she said, "My Mom doesn't like me rehearsing in my room. Dumb, huh?"

I didn't say anything.

"Probably it's 'cause I lock the door. Sometimes I just stay in there."

"Don't you get lonely?"

"Nope." Emily gave her thick brown hair a brave toss. She looked back at me. "Know what, Liz? I'm going to be a star. That's why I rehearse all the time. Then I can live in Hollywood, not dumb old here. Promise you'll come visit?"

"Sure, Emily. But I'd rather go riding with you in St. Andrews."

I heard her sigh.

"I guess living here might be fun. If he went away."

"Who?"

Emily wouldn't answer. Leaning forward, she urged Midnight into a trot, then a gallop. Lightning joined in the fun, and soon the horses were running side by side across an open field. The air was warm and sweet; wildflowers danced in the wind. Lightning tossed her head and snorted happily while her mane blew about my face. I could hear the rhythm of her hooves, pounding against the earth.

"This is fun," I yelled at Emily.

She grinned and waved.

During the ride, we saw the Road Beneath the Sea. "I'd never ride out there," Emily said. "What if the tide came in? Midnight would be trapped." Soon after, we reached a place where the sea came inland into a cove. "I've always wondered what's on the other side," Emily said, stopping Midnight at the water's edge.

"It's not too deep. The horses can walk across easily. Let's go explore," I urged.

As Lightning waded in, I looked back at Emily. She was gazing at the water.

"You'll be safe, Emily. You can do it."

She gazed thoughtfully at me. Then, lifting the reins, she took Midnight into the water. We started forward together. Midnight moved slowly, sensing Emily's anxiety. After several moments she stopped him.

"Liz, I . . ."

Before I could speak, Emily made Midnight back up. Turning back on Lightning, I joined them on shore.

Emily's eyes were huge. "The water, Liz. I . . ."

"Emily, you tried. That took courage."

She didn't say anything.

"I'm proud of you, Emily. I bet your Mom would be, too."

*　　　*　　　*

That evening, Makiko and I rode on Mrs. O'Neal's mountain bikes to the carnival outside of town. We wanted to follow up on our one good clue—the chunk of dried red mud we found at the scene of the abandoned house fire.

When we reached the carnival, we locked up our bikes and checked the earth around the entrance.

"The mud here is brown," Makiko said, holding the piece of red earth for comparison. "Van may not have come from here."

"Let's check inside."

"*Hey, hey, step right up,*" chanted a carny from his booth. "*Prizes here, prizes here,*" shouted another. The carnival was alive with people and noise and music from many different rides.

Everyone was eating junk food. I decided to get some cotton candy. "It always sticks to my face," I said to Makiko. "But I buy it every year."

She was busily eating onion rings. "These remind me of tempura," she said. "My parents have promised wonderful meals for your visit to Kyoto, Liz. Soon, I hope."

We searched the carnival, looking for the van, but had no luck. Walking through the midway, we checked the mud sample we'd brought along, but unfortunately the colors didn't match. "Let's try some rides," I said to Makiko. "At least the trip won't be a total waste."

As we headed toward the ferris wheel, I saw Drake. He was walking fast and looked troubled. "Let's follow him," I said. We moved quickly through the crowd in pursuit. Drake squeezed between two big trailers. We followed. He didn't seem to notice. He approached a semi with a large trailer attached. Painted in big letters on the side of the trailer were the words *Gizmo's Freak Show—Special Effects for All Occasions*.

Drake stepped with dignity over cables and dirty puddles, then knocked on the door of the trailer. The guy who answered had to be Gizmo. Ink from leaky pens had stained his shirt; his trousers stopped above his ankles. Gizmo's hair, thick as a wheatfield, stuck straight out. "He's put his fingers in too many sockets," I whispered to Makiko. "But he's no fool—those are shrewd eyes."

At that moment, a large, black motorcycle pulled up and roared to a stop. The rider looked mean in his Harley cap and shades. He had a thick moustache and a long braid of hair down his back. He wore torn jeans and his dusty boots were hung with chains.

"Hello, Rocky." Gizmo sneered at the biker. "Glad you could make it."

Rocky snorted in reply, then joined Drake and Gizmo at the door of the trailer. The men stood in a small circle, talking in whispers.

"Let's sneak closer," I whispered to Makiko.

We crept forward from trailer to trailer. My heart was thumping. The men were motioning wildly as they spoke. Without warning, the sunglasses shifted our way. Rocky's mouth opened in surprise. He pulled his Harley cap lower and turned his head, raising the collar of his leather jacket.

Drake and Gizmo stared at us. "Hey, you kids, go away," Drake ordered. "This is business."

"I wonder what Drake is up to?" I asked once we were back in the noisy crowd.

"Let us stay a while. Perhaps we shall see more," Makiko suggested. "In the meantime, let us try some of these rides."

On the midway, over-amplified rock music boomed from every side. While riders screamed above us on the Ring of Fire, we got tickets for the Gravitron. It spun us like a flying saucer; we were pressed against the wall by gravitational force. I was relieved when the ride ended.

Then we walked through the midway, and worked on some fries. They were thick and greasy. "Even with ketchup they're disgusting," I muttered. There were people all around us. Some wandered, staring, while others stood under awnings, playing the games. I tried to win a couple of giant neon-colored poodles by tossing baseballs into peach baskets, but I failed. "I never win anything," I complained. "Everything's rigged." But Makiko was awesome with a baseball, depositing one ball after another into the baskets. "You never told me," I said as she collected her pink poodle.

Smiling, she gave the prize to one of the watching kids. "Baseball is my favorite game. Father also. We avidly cheer the Hanshin Tigers."

Nibbling on popcorn, we watched the Bingo players, then talked to one of the orphans from *Annie*. "It's getting late," I said. "Shouldn't you be home?"

"I guess so," she replied, walking away. "I've been here since noon. I've eaten everything I can find, and I've been on every ride twice. See you."

Makiko and I went up on the ferris wheel. The view was breathtaking. The moon made a silver path across the ocean, and the stars dreamed in the night sky. I could have stayed forever.

"Liz, look!" Makiko pointed. "Perhaps this is what we were waiting for."

I followed Makiko's finger and saw Gizmo at the door of his trailer. He seemed nervous. He checked his watch, then looked around. I lost sight of him as the ferris wheel dipped down toward earth.

"We should investigate?" Makiko's eyes sparkled with pleasure.

Once the ferris wheel dropped us back on the ground, we hurried over to Gizmo's trailer. We watched Gizmo from the shadows as he secured the trailer for the night. Smoking a cigarette, he talked to some carnival workers. We heard swearing and noisy laughter. Beyond them, women and men played cards beside fires that burned inside trash barrels. Music continued to pound from the rides.

Then Gizmo left the others. He picked up a large sack and walked past the trailers and converted buses where the workers lived. We followed, hearing voices through open windows. As we turned a corner, Makiko stopped me. "Where is that man?"

I could see nothing but dark trailers. We tiptoed forward. Gizmo was gone; there was no sign of him. I saw empty fields beyond the carnival. Had he gone that way?

Then Gizmo leapt at us from hiding.

I screamed, and so did Makiko.

"You girls," Gizmo shouted into our faces. "Why are you watching me? You beat it, hear me? Get out of here!"

Makiko and I walked quickly away. I didn't look back until I felt safe. When I did, I saw Gizmo hurrying across a field.

"Let's see where he goes."

Makiko nodded. "But this time, let us stay farther back."

Gizmo climbed a stone fence into another empty field. We saw a shed that looked abandoned. Gizmo shoved the door open and disappeared inside. A light went on, glowing through a broken window.

We raced to the shed, then pressed close to the wall. In the light of the windows, Makiko compared some earth to our sample of red mud. "Same color," she whispered.

Gizmo's voice came through the broken window. "Yeah, yeah, I got the stuff."

A muffled grunt answered him.

"If you ask me, your whole scheme is crazy," Gizmo said. "But your boss is paying big bucks. You want my services, you got 'em."

I heard a door slam. An engine started with some difficulty, then a van towing a small trailer came out of the shed. The left tail-light was broken.

The van bumped away across the field. I looked at Makiko. "That was the van I saw at the fire!"

6

We watched until the headlights disappeared.

"Look at the time," I exclaimed. "FDR's expecting us."

We raced across the fields back to the carnival, where we pushed through the crowd. At the entrance, we found our bikes and were soon peddling through the night.

"Do you think we should tell police, Liz?"

"I told them about the van the night of the fire."

"But now we know it is van of Gizmo."

"We know Gizmo is in the van, but we don't know if he owns it. I wonder who was with him."

We found our way to FDR's house. It looked cosy, with

its curtained windows and wide porch, but no lights shone.

"It's odd the house is dark, when FDR is expecting us."

"*Ganbatte*," Makiko whispered.

"You're right." I gave her a weak smile. "We must press on." We opened a gate in the picket fence. Moonlight lay across the garden. We called FDR's name.

Nothing.

The front door was open.

"That's odd."

The hallway was in total darkness. I switched on a lamp. The wallpaper was patterned velvet; I saw a sofa and faded chairs in the living room. The furniture looked comfortable, and well used.

"Hello," I called. "FDR, we've come to visit."

Silence.

We glanced at each other. "I wish we'd brought a loaf of bread," I said. "That would show any spirits we mean no harm."

Then I heard a sound. *Tap. Tap. Tap.* My stomach tightened. I forced myself to move forward. What if FDR was in danger? I saw a library filled with books. Then a dining room with a wooden table, and candles in glass holders. The table had a lot of books on it.

Tap. Tap. Tap. The sound became louder. In the kitchen, the shelves had glass doors with porcelain handles. I saw big containers marked *flour* and *sugar*.

Makiko turned off a dripping faucet and the tapping sound ended. "Let's find the stairs," I said. "Something's wrong, but I don't know what."

There was one large room above. It was dominated by a grand piano. On the walls were autographed photos in elegant frames. I recognized some faces from the black-and-white Hollywood classics my parents love to watch on TV.

In front of a bay window was a large desk. It was scattered with papers and textbooks, and had a Canadian flag beside a paperweight filled with bubbles. I turned to Makiko. "Where's FDR?"

On a small coffee table was a tray with glasses of juice and pieces of cake, and a teapot. "It is warm," Makiko said. "FDR-san here recently."

"Why did he leave?"

I found a note sitting on the tray. "Look at this! It says, *Liz and Makiko, I'm at the Eagle's Nest.*" I studied the purple ink. "A lefty did this. See how the writing slopes?"

I looked at the Algonquin Hotel. Its large, black shape brooded above the town. "It's creepy without any lights," I said. "The hotel's empty because they're putting in new carpets and kitchens."

"Why would FDR go there?"

"I don't know, but I think we'd better go find out. He could be in danger."

Outside, clouds drifted across the moon. "Let's hope there isn't a fire," I said to Makiko. We looked at the night, seeking signs of smoke. Nothing moved but the trees, swaying softly in the wind.

As we walked toward the hotel, I thought of FDR and what Colby said about him at the theater. He seemed to be a nice man on the surface, but could he really be dangerous underneath?

"Know what a werewolf does?" I whispered. "It hypnotizes you, to make you believe it's your friend." I shuddered. "They roam at night, looking for victims."

Makiko touched her lips. "Please, Liz, no more of werewolf."

"You're right." I understood what she meant. I pointed into the night. "Look, Makiko! *What's that?*"

*   *   *

Up by the entrance of the hotel, the moonlight showed a creature. Its face had scary red eyes, a snout and jagged teeth. It looked like some kind of animal, covered in black fur, but it stood on its hind legs. We heard a fearful howling, then the thing rushed away.

Makiko stared at me. "Werewolf!"

"No," I said. "It's a disguise, I'm sure of it." I grabbed her arm. "It ran toward the hotel. Come on, let's follow it."

We hurried across a wide lawn toward a two-storey building on the grounds of the hotel. The creature had disappeared into the shadows of the building. I switched on my pocket flashlight. We found an open door, and stepped into a hallway. To our right, we saw another open door which led to a set of dark stairs.

We followed the stairs down to a tunnel. "This must connect to the hotel," I said. "Let's follow it."

Our footsteps made the only noise as we crept through the dark tunnel. But our steps echoed, making the hair on my neck stand on end. I swept my flashlight across the darkness. My light showed nothing. "Come on," I whispered.

We moved along the tunnel cautiously. Water dripped around us. When we emerged, we found ourselves in a hallway that had large doors on both sides.

"There's the kitchen." I flashed my light into the enormous work space. Gigantic jars of mustard, pickles and relish stood in rows and the shelves were full of pots and pans.

Something moved in the darkness. I flashed my light in time to see a jar tilting on a shelf. It hung for a moment, then fell. The glass smashed on the floor with a terrible sound. Makiko and I grabbed each other and screamed.

Another jar fell. This time, I saw the creature pushing it. Snarling, the creature dashed out through a door at the far end of the kitchen. We raced after it into a hallway. At the end of the hall, we saw the thing reach a spiral staircase.

Up it ran, up into the darkness of the tower. We both took a breath, murmured *Ganbatte* and went after it. The tower stairs were very old. They creaked as we climbed carefully. I probed the murky air with my flashlight.

At the end of our climb was the Eagle's Nest. Moonlight poured through the windows. The creature watched us, hunched in the corner. Beside him, a candle burned in an old-fashioned lantern. The creature took the candle out and lit a small pile of papers.

"No!" I screamed.

The flames leaped up quickly, licking at the dry wooden wall.

With a low growl, the creature rushed through a door on the opposite side and down the stairs. I started in pursuit, then realized we had to put out the fire. The flames were hot on my face as I looked for something to smother them with.

"Stand back." Makiko had a fire extinguisher in her hand. "It was on wall outside." She directed the spray onto the flames. The fire was out in no time.

*   *   *

The climb down those creaking wooden stairs was scary. I kept expecting the creature to leap out at us, but nothing happened. We wandered through the hallways, seeking an exit. In the lower hallway, we saw furniture covered with large sheets, stacks of lumber and many containers of paint.

"What do you think, Makiko? If that was a disguise, who was inside?"

"I do not know, but this was not creature we saw on island."

"No, but that looked like its lantern."

We went outside. The wind felt good on my face. We had just started walking along Prince of Wales Drive when we ran into FDR. He was staggering along the road. "My head," he moaned, clutching it. "I feel so horrible."

"What happened?" I exclaimed.

"I was at home, waiting for your arrival. The phone rang. A man said to meet him at the Algonquin Hotel. I left immediately after I hung up."

"You didn't stop for anything?"

"No." FDR seemed quite surprised. "He made it sound so urgent."

"Who was the man?"

"I didn't recognize the voice. It was muffled, as if he was trying to disguise it. He threatened my house with arson unless I met him at the hotel's pavilion. I was waiting beside it in the darkness when, all of a sudden, stars exploded inside my skull. I woke up a few minutes ago, with a terrible headache."

I studied FDR's face. His pain seemed real, but he did come from a family of actors.

From out of nowhere, Colby came jogging up. "I see everyone is out enjoying the evening," he said, winking at me.

When we told him about the attack on FDR, Colby pulled out a cellular phone and called the police. When they arrived, I heard FDR's story again. It remained consistent.

The police left, taking FDR along for further questioning. Colby volunteered to walk us home.

"It's odd," I said. "FDR told me he left immediately for the hotel after he received the phone call. I wonder why he didn't mention writing the note?"

"Perhaps FDR-san seeks to deceive?" Makiko suggested. "Attack faked by himself?"

"Be very cautious around FDR," Colby warned. "Sure, he seems meek and mild with his glasses and his books. But I've heard rumors he's dangerous."

"Weird, isn't it?" I said. "I'd better ask FDR some questions. I'd like to know what he knows about Gizmo."

"Gizmo?" Colby asked. "Who is Gizmo?"

I told him about what we had seen at the carnival. Colby listened carefully. "But you don't really know whether the person in the van started the fire. It could just be a coincidence that the van was there when the fire broke out that night," he said thoughtfully.

"That's true," I said. I looked back at the shadow-washed Algonquin Hotel. There were so many missing pieces to the puzzle.

That night, as I lay in bed, many thoughts went through my mind. I had a lot of questions to ask tomorrow, and a few things to find out.

*　　*　　*

The next morning, I went back to the Old Gaol. I wanted to check the birth records for the last twenty years. I found the entry I was looking for. I made a note of it. I needed to check something else out, but it would have to wait until later.

On our way to the theater, Makiko and I passed a *Yes Mall* rally. Drake was there, giving a speech. There was a band, and free hot dogs and soft drinks.

"Boy, Drake's really gone all out," I said, as I watched a hundred red and white helium balloons fly up into the sky. "He really wants the mall to happen. I guess he'd do anything to see it built."

"Is that not Gizmo?" Makiko asked. I looked into the crowd. There was no mistaking that hair.

"He sure seems interested in the mall."

"Maybe he just wants free hot dog," Makiko giggled.

"Hey, Liz," someone called. I turned and saw Colby— brilliant blue eyes, gorgeous smile and all. He joined us. "The support for the mall is growing. It looks like it may end up a tie vote."

*　　*　　*

The orphans were rehearsing their opening number when we entered the theater. There was a woman backstage watching from the wings. I recognized her as Emily's mom.

Emily ran over to me as soon as the song was over. Her face was all aglow. I had never seen her so excited.

"Guess what, Liz? I crossed the cove today on Midnight. I did it!"

"Wow, Emily. That's marvelous."

Emily's mother laughed with pleasure. "She couldn't wait to tell you. You're very nice to Emily. Every day she can't wait to go to the theater." She smiled fondly at her child.

"She's a really excellent actor," I said. "She seems to come alive when she's on stage."

"I was wondering if you and Makiko would like to come over to our house after rehearsal today. I made cho . . ."

"Chocolate cake!" I exclaimed.

Her face fell. "No, I made chopped liver."

As I stared at her in dismay, she smiled. "Fooled you.

Emily said you and Makiko like chocolate cake, so I made one."

"We'd love to come," I said. "Thanks, Emily."

Emily had become quiet and withdrawn. "It was my mother's idea."

Just then, Colin called the Rockettes to take their places on the stage. I hastened over and joined the rest of the dancers. The music started. I took my stance and all my energy went into performing.

The rehearsal went quickly. I was so busy with my various roles that I hardly noticed anything else. But I did note that FDR didn't show up for rehearsal. There were a lot of rumors being whispered about him on the stage.

After rehearsal, Makiko and I walked with Emily to her home. Emily wanted to show us her room and all her things. "I've built a really cool home for my dolls," she said. "I made it all by myself."

As we approached the house, we were greeted by the sound of yapping and barking. Emily halted. "That's our new dog."

"What's his name?"

"Max," she said, "but I don't like him."

Emily's mother met us at the door. She held the dog by the collar so he wouldn't jump. Emily seemed afraid of the dog. She kept her distance from him as she entered the house.

The chocolate cake was delicious. Emily's mom could really bake. When we had finished eating, Emily showed us her doll house, her model horse collection and all her books. "Do you want to play Chinese jump rope?" she asked.

"Sure," we both said.

"Don't be too late," her mother told us as we went out the door. "Your father will be home soon."

Emily became quiet all of a sudden. Her face went pale. "Stepfather," she corrected.

Makiko, Emily, and I played Chinese jump rope in the backyard. Emily was winning. Her face was flushed and happy.

"Emily," a man's voice called.

Emily looked up. She turned suddenly afraid.

Her stepfather stood in the back doorway. He had Max with him. The short-haired mongrel was pulling hard against the leash.

"Emily! Isn't it one of your chores to walk Max?"

She didn't say anything. Her eyes were on the ground, and her hands trembled.

"Emily, we've got this new dog. You must take your turn walking it." He held out the leash. "Trust me, you won't get hurt."

"I'm afraid," she whispered.

"You must do as I tell you, Emily." His eyes were very blue. "It's your duty to walk the dog."

"I never wanted to get it. I'm scared of dogs." She looked up at the man. "Last time, it ran away from me and chased someone. You got mad."

"I won't be angry ever again," he replied. "I promise."

"What if it hurts me?"

"It won't, Emily. I'll never let you get hurt."

Slowly, she held out her hand for the leash. The dog was straining forward, anxious for its walk. The man put Emily's hand into the loop on the leash, and then let go.

Right away, the dog sprang forward. Emily was caught off balance, and fell hard. The cement ripped her knees, and I saw blood. Emily dropped the leash, crying. The dog immediately took off running.

The man swore angrily at Emily, then ran after the dog. It was already in the neighbor's garden, happily digging up flowers. The man looked guiltily in the window of the house, then grabbed the dog and ran back to Emily.

"More trouble," he said, glancing anxiously about. "Come on, Emily, let's go inside. Any more problems with this dog, and I'll get sued." He helped Emily to her feet, and brushed the pebbles from her torn knees. "Listen, it's our secret about the garden getting dug up, okay? Don't tell, or everything will be terrible. Emily has to go inside now," her stepfather informed us. "Thank you for dropping by."

Emily threw us a look of grief as she was led inside.

7

I was nervous about attending the first dress rehearsal for *Annie*. But I felt better when I saw the spectacular costumes. Dancing as a Rockette, I'd be wearing a top hat and a sequined tuxedo that shimmered under the bright spotlights.

Colin called Makiko up on stage to present her with an *Annie* souvenir sweatshirt. While everyone applauded, Makiko wriggled into the sweatshirt and bowed her thanks.

Colby used spirit gum to attach Elvis sideburns to his face, then sang "Heartbreak Hotel" to Makiko and the orphans. Everyone adored him. After that, Margaret, the music director, warmed up our voices with the show's hit song, "Tomorrow." I felt wonderful. We were like a family.

Then we heard wheels rolling onto the stage. Everyone turned to see FDR in the wooden wheelchair. Light flashed from his spectacles.

"I couldn't miss rehearsal again," he said. "I hope I'm welcome."

"Of course," Colin exclaimed.

Before long, we were under the lights, in full costume. The girl who played Annie was home with the flu, so Emily took the role. She was terrific.

Eventually, we took a break. At the pop machine, the orphans all talked at once about the hotel fire, FDR and the werewolf. People were beginning to think that the legend of the St. Andrews werewolf might be true after all.

"I told you FDR was the werewolf," Tegan said to me.

"You don't have any proof."

"Yes, we do. He started the fire at the hotel. Everyone knows the werewolf is the arsonist."

"That's right," Ashlee added. "And he goes to Minister's Island, dresses as a werewolf, then comes over and burns our houses."

"Why would he do that?" I asked.

The orphans couldn't agree on an answer to my question.

"I'd like a little more proof. There are a few things I want to check out before I jump to any conclusions."

Emily kept avoiding me. After she had finished practicing her big number, I took her aside. "Please thank your Mom again for the chocolate cake, okay?"

"Sure." Her brown eyes stared at the floor.

"It's great you crossed the cove on Midnight, Emily. You're getting really courageous."

A smile flitted across her face. "It was easier than I thought."

"You were dynamite on stage today."

Colin stopped beside us. "We see more of your talent every rehearsal, Emily. You're like a flower, slowly blossoming."

She scuffed her foot against the stage. "Thank you, Colin."

"Thinking of a career in show biz?"

She nodded shyly. "But how do I get ready?"

"Read about theater at the library. Always believe in yourself, because you won't get every role you audition for. Rejection can hurt."

"Colin," I asked, "how did you get your start? Was it difficult?"

He smiled. "I started as a beginner, just like everyone else. I was scared but determined. I learned my craft, and I was curious. Understanding people sharpens the actor." Colin paused. "It also helps with real-life problems. Sometimes my feelings get hurt. I always ask myself why it happened. Was the other person having a bad day, or maybe feeling jealous? That way, I don't always think it's my fault."

As Emily asked a question, I was almost run over by FDR. "I'm still having trouble with this wheelchair," he apologized.

"No problem. FDR, may I ask you a question?"

"Fire away."

"What would you do if you had a lot of money?"

FDR smiled. "I'd live out my dream."

"What's your dream?"

He smiled shyly. "A charitable foundation with a differ-ence—a panel of kids would decide how to spend the money. Anyone could suggest a project to receive funds. For example, someone in St. Andrews might ask the foundation to buy land for a park. Or maybe scholarships for needy kids to go to university. So much could be done!"

"I like it," I said as Colin called for the rehearsal to continue. "Oh, could you write down your address again? I've lost it."

"Sure thing." FDR fished out a fountain pen. "This was presented to my parents by Irving Berlin. Dad always claimed that Mr. Berlin used it to compose his big hit, 'White Christmas.'"

Using his right hand, FDR wrote down his address.

"Thanks," I said. I studied his writing. The elegant script slanted evenly to the right. I folded the paper and slipped it into my pocket.

*   *   *

"All this talk about werewolf makes me worry." Makiko's pretty face was pulled into a frown. "The creature we saw at Eagle's Nest was not creature we saw on island. But now people think werewolf on island is arsonist."

"What's your theory?"

"I think someone is trying to make a frame," she concluded.

I agreed. "But who is framing whom?" I asked.

"Perhaps FDR-san is using creature to scare people."

"Somebody is, but I still don't know for sure if it's FDR." I showed her the sample of FDR's writing and compared it to the note we found at his house. The handwriting was different.

"He could have disguised it." Makiko said.

Although I was pretty sure FDR was not the arsonist, I couldn't rule him out altogether. I knew the only place we could clear up most of this mystery was at Coven Hoven. What was its secret? I told Makiko what I had discovered about the old Van Horne mansion in my last visit to the archives.

"We must go back to the island," Makiko urged.

"I know," I shuddered. I wasn't exactly looking forward to the trip.

*   *   *

That afternoon, we borrowed a couple of kayaks from Fran. After a little practice, we set out toward the island.

The wind was from the north. The air was cold and fresh on my skin. Far above, black clouds were driven across the sky as if by unseen forces. It felt as if a storm was coming. I hoped it would hold off until we returned.

Gliding swiftly through the ocean waters, we approached Minister's Island. "Let's beach the kayaks near the Road Beneath the Sea," I called to Makiko.

Mustard-colored moss covered the big rocks along the shore. Enormous signs shouted *Private Property* and *Keep Out*. "I don't feel very welcome," I said to Makiko.

I looked for the Road Beneath the Sea, but the tide was in and it was covered by water. Powerful currents swirled through the narrow strait. We found a place to beach our kayaks. We stumbled across a rocky beach, then climbed a slope to rolling fields that were brilliantly green. The air was sweet, and wildflowers danced in the wind.

"Regard barn," Makiko said. "So excellent!"

It was the biggest I'd ever seen. The walls were high, topped by an enormous roof. On top was a weather vane shaped like a cow. High on the barn, a row of windows looked down like frowning eyes.

My heart beat fast as we entered the barn through a huge doorway. Swallows darted past us into the sunshine.

The barn was almost empty. Beside a wall was some rusty farm equipment, and an ancient fire engine designed to be pulled by horses. Above us was a wooden loft.

"I think I just heard footsteps." I studied the ceiling, wondering how to get up there. I listened carefully, then shook my head. "Maybe I'm wrong. I could have heard raccoons in the walls."

"Let us investigate."

We studied the loft above us. "There's got to be a way up to that part of the barn," I said. "But I can't see it."

"I see stairs." Makiko pointed into a dusty corner. "But they go down."

We followed the stairs to the barn's lower floor. The stalls were all empty, but something caught my eye. "Hey, Makiko, there's some fresh oats." I recalled the figure escaping from the Burying Ground. "Remember, the creature had a white stallion."

"I am afraid for this creature," Makiko said as we returned upstairs. I grabbed Makiko's arm and squeezed a warning. Someone stood in the shadows near the old fire engine.

8

A man stepped out of the shadows. His head was totally bald. A ratty little grey beard grew from his chin. He had small, shifty eyes. His face was creased by lines. He wore a long white coat, gloves and boots. He looked at least seventy, maybe older.

"My name is Smart." His voice was thin. He studied me, then Makiko. "You are trespassing on private property. Shall I notify the police? Or shall I imprison you both in a basement dungeon?"

"We've come with a warning," I said urgently. "Do you work for Lady Chandler? Someone is trying to frame the creature who lives on this island. They are blaming it for all the arson. He or she might be in danger."

Smart sniffed. "Absolute rubbish." He pointed to the door. "Get off this island immediately. Never return."

"We were only trying to help," I protested. "You're not being fair."

A voice spoke from the shadows. "The young lady is correct. Apologize to her, Smart."

A very elegant older woman walked toward us. "I'm Lady Chandler." Her voice was deep and rich. Her clothes were eccentric and out-of-date. Her snow-white hair was piled in a bun. Her eyes were black and intelligent. They studied us.

"I appreciate the warning, young ladies. Smart has been very rude. He will now apologize."

His little eyes gave her a look I couldn't read. "Sorry," he mumbled insincerely.

We introduced ourselves to Lady Chandler as we left the barn. Waiting outside was a beautiful horse hitched to a shiny carriage. "Climb up," Lady Chandler ordered. "We're going to Coven Hoven for tea. I haven't had company for years."

Smart glanced at us, then grabbed the reins. Soon we were flying past the tall grass. All around were daisies, clover, and Queen Anne's lace. "The clover makes the hay more sweet for the cows," Lady Chandler said. "In the days of Sir William Van Horne, there were eighty head of Clydesdale cattle in the barn. Sir William didn't want his workers daydreaming, so he put the windows too high to look out. Every night, they traced Van Horne's coat-of-arms in sawdust freshly spread on the barn floor. The workers wore overalls and lab coats—Smart deliberately copies the outfit. We both love this island, and we know its entire history. Did you know that Van Horne wanted to live for five hundred years?"

"Did he make it?" I asked.

Lady Chandler laughed at the joke. "He tried, but unfortunately not. He could be quite a quack, though. He sometimes kept a potato in his pocket to ward off rheumatism."

"How did Minister's Island get its name?" I asked.

"The first person to own the island was a clergyman."

"In school, I have studied about Van Horne-san. Famous man for building famous railway," Makiko said.

"He knew how to get things done, and he had a zest for life. Sir William expected nothing but perfection." Lady Chandler smiled. "I'm afraid I'm talking too much. It's just so nice to have company."

"You should do it more often, Lady Chandler."

She stiffened. "Unfortunately, it is not possible. I invited you girls for tea because you're strangers. You'll leave St. Andrews by summer's end. You won't pester me for visits, and then snoop around. Others have tried that. It hurt me deeply. I told Smart to seal off this island. He has been very successful."

"You're right," I said. "The kids in town are terrified of this place. It seems a shame, when it's such a beautiful island. Couldn't you open it up, maybe just for kids?"

"They wouldn't understand."

"But what's the problem, Lady Chandler? Is a treasure buried here?"

"A treasure, yes, but not one anyone would want. This island is private property, and will remain so. I cherish my privacy."

"Well, we're sure honored to be invited for tea."

Makiko bowed her head. "Such a delight."

Ahead of us loomed the mansion, Coven Hoven. It was tremendous, stretching in many directions. There were many chimneys and countless windows. "It has eleven bathrooms, and two hundred and fourteen doorknobs," Lady Chandler said. "I've counted them."

Smart stopped the carriage at the front door. Climbing down, I sniffed some pretty roses that grew by the house. "The creature left roses like these on the grave."

"What creature?"

"The one we saw on this island, Lady Chandler."

"You must never use that word again. How horrid!"

When we entered the mansion, we stepped back in time. The place was filled with chandeliers, oil portraits and mahogany furniture. Candlelight glowed in mirrors that filled entire walls. A gold clock ticked on the mantel of a huge fireplace.

"It's like being in another time," I exclaimed.

A ghost of a smile crossed Lady Chandler's lips. She tapped a beautiful rug with her cane. "This was years in the making, entirely by hand. It's irreplaceable." She pointed at two curious chairs. "Those are camel chairs. My husband was independently wealthy. He became a doctor and served the people of Egypt. We retired to Canada twenty years ago, purchased Coven Hoven and restored its glories to the days of Van Horne."

Lady Chandler led us toward a staircase. "Let me show you the upper floor."

It was like a maze upstairs. Hallways zigged and zagged in all directions. "Is your bedroom up here, Lady Chandler?"

"No, I sleep downstairs. This is too gloomy for me."

"Are there ghosts?"

"One night, I thought I heard footsteps up here. Smart

and I investigated. The footsteps came close to us, then vanished. The air became extremely cold." For several moments, she said nothing. "I've never heard them again."

"Wow," I said. "Creepy."

I noticed all the bedroom doors were open, except for one. "What's in here?" I asked.

"Don't," Lady Chandler exclaimed. She grabbed my hand before I could open the door.

"Sorry," I said.

Downstairs, I saw a comfortable-looking room with a big TV set. Pretty flowers stood in big vases. Two big sofas faced a wall of electronic equipment. I looked at the CDs and laser discs. "This is really great music you listen to, Lady Chandler. You're really into rock music, eh?"

She didn't reply.

We followed Lady Chandler through Coven Hoven, eventually reaching the living room. It was the size of a small air terminal. We sat on a velvety chesterfield, surrounded by soft pillows. Smart appeared from a distant kitchen carrying a silver tray. On it was a tea service that looked like Royal Doulton.

"The tea smells delicious," I said.

"Huh," Smart muttered.

When he was gone, Lady Chandler passed us plates of buttered bread. "Bread for friendship," she said. I nibbled some, but saved my appetite for the carrot cake with super-thick icing waiting for us on the tray.

"This is fantastic, Lady Chandler. Your friends must love staying here."

"I have no friends. I have no guests."

"But you live here with your husband, don't you?"

"He died recently, God rest his soul."

Sighing, Lady Chandler lowered herself into a sofa by the fireplace. She picked up a leather-bound book. "Do you know about Mary Shelley? Long ago, she was married to a famous poet. While still a teenager, she wrote this book called *Frankenstein*."

"I've seen the movie," I said. "Boris Karloff was excellent."

Lady Chandler looked at us. The firelight deepened the lines around her eyes. "The agony of that unhappy brute," she said, "shunned by the world. The cruelty of people!"

"Frankenstein was just a story, Lady Chandler. Besides, these are modern times. My friends don't think it's fun to cause pain."

Her eyes flashed at me. "But it could happen! What then? Frightened people can be so cruel."

There was a loud crash of thunder.

"It's a storm," Makiko said, looking out the window at the tossing ocean. "How will we get back home?"

"I'm afraid you'll have to stay the night," Lady Chandler said. "I'll tell Smart to set two more places for dinner."

I phoned Fran to let her know we were all right and that we had been invited to stay at Coven Hoven. "Take notes," she said. "I'd give anything to visit that place."

*   *   *

When I came downstairs for dinner, I was still wearing my jeans. I wish I had worn something nicer, but then, I hadn't expected this invitation. In the big hallway, Smart sat alone at an organ, playing mournful sounds. He glared at me.

"Don't ever come back to Coven Hoven," he hissed, continuing to play the depressing music.

I tried to smile, pretending Smart didn't make me nervous.

Makiko came downstairs, looking beautiful even in jeans. Lady Chandler waited in the dining room. The candlelight was soft, casting an eerie glow on the many paintings.

Lady Chandler sat at the head of the table. I sat on one side of her, Makiko on the other. The rest of the table was empty, although twenty more people could have comfortably joined us.

"I once had happy times at this table," Lady Chandler said. "My son and his wife lived here. The house rang with their laughter."

"What happened, Lady Chandler?" I asked softly.

"They died. In a motor crash here on the island. There was a bad storm. My son drove too fast and crashed into a tree. There was a terrible fire." Lady Chandler looked up at an oil portrait. It showed a handsome young man, his wife and a little boy. "Since their deaths, I have forbidden motor cars on Minister's Island."

"What happened to the little boy?"

A spasm of pain contorted Lady Chandler's face. "He died, too. I adored him."

"Wallace," I said.

Lady Chandler looked surprised. "How do you know?"

"I ran across an article in the town archives about your family."

"Please, don't mention his name again. Let the dead lie in peace."

Makiko gently touched Lady Chandler's hand. "I have great feeling for you, Chandler-san."

She smiled gratefully. "Thank you, my dear. It's good to have you visiting Coven Hoven. Your generation has strength and optimism. My generation has wisdom. If only the young and old could combine forces, we'd make a better world." She opened her napkin. "Now, we must eat."

Smart produced a salmon that was absolutely delicious. We worked on it while talking. Lady Chandler kept us entertained with stories of her life in Egypt. She also told us about how she and her late husband worked to restore Coven Hoven.

"This place is like a living museum," Makiko said.

"Yes," Lady Chandler mused, lost in thought. "But what will happen when I die? That's my greatest worry."

"You're concerned about the future of the island, Lady Chandler?"

"No, about . . ."

She was interrupted by Smart, who arrived with dessert. I tried to encourage her to say more, but she grew silent. "I am tired," she said. "Having company has been exhilarating, and exhausting. I must go to my bed."

Upstairs later, I sat at my window brushing my hair and looking at the moonlight on the sea. The storm had died down and the night was quiet.

I crawled into bed, and tried unsuccessfully to sleep. Around midnight, the silence was broken by the sound of distant music. Somebody was playing the guitar. I heard it clearly. Going into the hallway, I met Makiko. Cautiously, we followed the music along the hallway. We reached the door that had been closed during our tour with Lady Chandler. As I opened the door, it squealed on its hinges.

The sound was a warning to someone inside. I heard the scramble of feet on the roof. I rushed to the open window, but could see nothing.

"Let us go to another window," Makiko suggested.

Quickly, we raced back to my room. We scanned the

dark night, hoping to get a glimpse of something. A figure emerged out of the darkness, carrying a heavy lantern. It was just like the one the werewolf had at the Eagle's Nest.

"Can you see who it is, Liz?"

"Yes." My heart filled with dismay. "It's FDR."

Smart stepped outside, and stood talking to FDR. We couldn't hear their words. Smart handed FDR an envelope. FDR took it and left. Suddenly, Smart looked up and caught us watching. He shook his fist and went inside.

I tried to sleep again, but my thoughts kept me awake. Over and over I asked myself the same question—was FDR really the arsonist?

9

The next morning, Lady Chandler stayed in her room. Smart gave us breakfast, but wouldn't let us say goodbye to Lady Chandler. I wanted to ask her about FDR. I started to question Smart, but that was a lost cause.

Smart drove us in the carriage to the gate. "Don't ever come back," he said.

I straightened my spine. "Goodbye, Smart. It's been a slice."

Makiko giggled.

It was a great trip home in the kayaks. Morning mist lay across the ocean waters. The waves moved gently, turning blue, then green. Birds chased each other, crying out in delight.

Fran was waiting for me when I got back. I told her everything I had learned about Coven Hoven as we sat drinking cups of herbal tea.

"It's a shame she keeps that place hidden," Fran sighed.

Just then, Makiko arrived to accompany me to the theater.

"I have had a long telephone conversation with my family. Each sends affectionate regards to you, Liz."

"Thanks!"

Before we left, Fran had some news for us. "Drake has just offered Greta O'Neal's son a job as manager at the mall. He wouldn't have to leave town. I don't think we could say anything now that would make her vote against the mall."

"Would Mrs. O'Neal let herself be bribed like that?"

"I don't know. I thought I knew her pretty well. But this is a tough decision."

I gave Fran a hug. "Don't forget. The fireworks start at sunset," Fran said.

"How could I forget? I love Canada Day celebrations."

*   *   *

Makiko and I walked through town on our way to the theater. Canadian flags were everywhere waving in the breeze. Red and white streamers festooned lamp posts. "It is so festive," Makiko laughed.

Colby joined us, carrying hot dogs. "Your favorite," he said to Makiko. Colby looked at his watch. "Another dress rehearsal today."

We bought ice cream cones, and ate them on our way. The salty sea air mingled with the fragrance of freshly mowed grass. I waved at Mrs. O'Neal. She was on her porch, listening to someone who was talking and gesturing wildly.

"That person must be talking about the mall," I said. "Poor Mrs. O'Neal. Everyone's trying to influence her."

"She'll vote yes," Colby predicted.

"Mrs. O'Neal will vote for what is best for the town," I replied strongly.

We arrived at the theater and Colby went straight toward his dressing room with a quick, "See you."

Backstage, the theater people discussed the vote as they got into costume and applied their makeup. "I don't like the mall," Miss Hannigan said, leaning toward the mirror with a stick of greasepaint. Bright lightbulbs surrounded her face. "If I owned that land, I'd donate it for a park. Who wants some giant mall in our backyard?"

"I do," one of the singers, Barbara, said. "This place needs jobs—I don't want my boyfriend leaving town."

"Somebody is using some pretty strong methods to force Greta O'Neal to vote for the mall," Miss Hannigan said. "If you know what I mean."

I wandered out to the stage, where Emily found me. "Guess what?" she exclaimed. "Mom and I went riding at night, all the way to the Road Beneath the Sea. Next I'm going to try it alone."

I gave her a hug. "You're getting really courageous."

Drake approached in his butler outfit. He wore a gold watch chain across his stomach, and little pince-nez glasses over his snobby eyes. "Have you seen Colby?" he asked.

"Not since I arrived," I answered.

"I have to find him," Drake muttered gruffly and then stomped away. Emily scurried across stage to join Miss Hannigan and the other orphans for notes from Colin.

I sat by myself on stage. FDR rolled toward me in his wooden chair. "Hi Liz. Found anything more on the arsonist?"

I shook my head. "Makiko and I have some clues."

"I hope they catch him. He's destroying the town."

"I agree," I said. "FDR, what were you doing at Coven Hoven last night?"

"What?! I wasn't there."

"I saw you."

FDR's smile disappeared and his face became stern. "I think you are mistaken," he said and rolled away.

I was upset. Why was FDR lying to me?

But once I was on stage, I felt better. I finally stopped worrying about when to say my lines—they had become second nature to me. So I relaxed. I forgot about everything that was troubling me. All I thought about was the play. After the opening number, I suddenly believed that *Annie* was real life instead of a make-believe story. It was a magic moment. The rehearsal became really fun. I did a great solo tap in the radio scene.

After the performance, Colin gathered us in the empty seats of the theater for cast notes. Colby came up and seemed to be in a better mood than before. We sat together during the notes, holding hands.

Colby offered to go with me to the Canada Day fireworks at the Point. "Great," I said, "but I'm going to Fran's after for hot chocolate."

"Maybe I'll convince you otherwise," he said with a wink. "Give me a minute—I've got a message for Drake."

I waited in the lobby with Makiko. Time passed slowly. Colby was gone for about ten minutes, and seemed jittery when he returned. "Drake is in a terrible mood," he said, as we left the theater. "He's totally stressed about the vote."

*   *   *

A big crowd of townspeople and tourists had gathered at an outdoor concert stage at the Point. We sang "O Canada" as pink clouds drifted above Passamaquoddy Bay. We were like a family together, a community in harmony with nature. I looked around, wanting the best for everyone. Emily was in the crowd with her mother. They both gave me timid smiles.

After the anthem, the ceremonies and entertainment began. A wild Maritimes band played jigs and reels while everyone danced and clapped along. "It's getting dark," Colby said, spinning me in a dance. "At last."

"You really like fireworks, don't you?" I asked.

He grinned. "You could say that."

The night turned crimson as the first firebomb exploded above us. The crowd went *ooooh* as silver stars burst in bright patterns, then *aaaah* as pinwheels spun in rainbows of colors.

Makiko grinned at me. "Such a happy evening, Liz."

Just then I felt a small hand in mine. I looked down at Emily. "I don't want to go home," she said. "I want to stay with you."

Her mother came out of the crowd. "Emily, we have to go."

"I don't want to." Emily's hand squeezed tighter. "Let me stay with you. Please."

I looked at her mother. "Fran's invited some friends for a girl's night at her place. Maybe Emily could join us for hot chocolate, then Fran could drive her home."

Emily's eyes glowed. "Yes!"

Her mother smiled. "Very well, sweetheart. But straight home after."

"Okay, Mom."

I turned to Colby. "Maybe I'll see you tomorrow."

"You're going to this hot chocolate thing instead of being with me? Skip it, okay? Stay with me."

"This is important to Emily," I said, "and to me."

Colby shook his head. "Okay, Liz. I'll see you later." He walked away, shoulders slumped. Emily's hand was still in mine, and I knew I'd done the right thing, but I was a bit glum anyway.

*   *   *

"Cheer up," Fran said as the crowd walked back to town from the Point. We were with two other friends of Fran. One was Miss Hannigan from our musical. "You've got to look below the surface," Fran said. "Handsome is as handsome does."

"What do you mean?" I asked.

"Judge a person by who they are on the inside, not how they look on the outside."

"I know that," I sighed. "But I guess I fell for a pretty face."

"It may all work out." Fran patted my shoulder.

"I don't know. I really don't like his attitude."

At Seaside Cabins, I went to my little place—"Sandpiper"—with Emily for sweaters. She studied every detail of the one room with its tiny attached bathroom. "Did you bring this little jade elephant from Winnipeg?"

I nodded. "It's a present from my uncle and aunt. It goes everywhere with me. I keep it facing the door for protection. It's kind of a superstition, I guess."

"I should get one," Emily said. "Sometimes when I'm falling asleep, I picture a fairy princess going room to room with her wand, making things better." She sighed. "Last night I had a weird dream. I was holding a flower. It was so pretty and fragile, and I was trying to protect it."

"From what?"

Emily shrugged. "I forget."

Her eyes looked scared, so I gave her a hug. "Let's go get some hot chocolate."

We walked together toward the sea. A bonfire glowed on the faces of Fran, Makiko and the others. *Fire's burning, fire's burning*, they sang, *draw nearer, draw nearer*.

The singing was led by Savanna, a friend of Fran's. After a few of my favorite songs, Fran told a ghost story. We roasted marshmallows, then Fran poured refills of hot chocolate. "Such a peaceful night," she said, looking up at the stars.

Savanna began talking about her niece. "She says that things have been happening to her. I know who the man is, and I don't like him. But I think she's making too much of it."

Miss Hannigan looked at her. "Are you talking about sexual abuse?"

"Yes."

"What's she said?"

Savanna told her the details. Miss Hannigan listened carefully, then said, "That girl means it."

"You sound so certain."

"I *am* certain." Miss Hannigan looked at the flames, then at Savanna. "You see, it happened to me."

Emily's hand clutched mine more tightly. I looked at her, wondering if she should be listening to the conversation. I got up to leave, intent on taking her away from the gathering.

"No," Miss Hannigan said. "Let Emily stay." She looked around at the circle of faces. "I felt guilty not trusting someone who said he loved me. My mother loved me, and I trusted her. My father said he loved me and he'd never hurt me, but he *was* hurting me. In my heart, I knew I couldn't trust him."

Fran took Miss Hannigan's hand, and held it.

"I had to get over feeling guilty about this," Miss Hannigan said, "and do something to save myself. So I told. It wasn't easy, but I did it. My Mom wasn't angry. She cried, and she hugged me, and she got us help."

Miss Hannigan stirred the flames with a stick. Glowing sparks danced up into the night. "My counsellors were good people. I'd thought everyone knew about it, but people don't have x-ray vision. They can't see inside your head. That's why my Mom never guessed. It was right to tell the secret because my father was lying. The secret hurt me, and it protected him."

Miss Hannigan looked at us. "After I told, I felt safer. I knew it wasn't my fault it happened." She patted Fran's hand. "Things slowly got better, and today I'm so happy that little girl told the secret. She gave a precious gift to the woman I am. She gave me pride. No one has power over me."

Everyone was silent for a moment. Fran put an arm around Miss Hannigan, who quickly wiped a tear from her eye. "Thanks for listening to me, everyone." Miss Hannigan smiled.

"Thank *you*," Savanna said. "I'm going to pay attention to my niece."

Nobody said much as the party ended. Emily and I helped cover the fire's burning embers, then she climbed into Fran's 4x4 to go home. "Thanks, Liz," Emily said quietly from the window. "You're my best friend."

10

The next evening, I was at the pier with Makiko. After a long day at rehearsal, we were celebrating with an ice cream cone before attending the vote on the mall. "Let's get there soon," I said, consulting my watch. "The place will be packed."

On a wall inside the Charlotte County Courthouse were the portraits of the king and queen, and their thirteen kids, who'd been honored when St. Andrews was founded. "This place has been in use since 1840," I read out from a tourist brochure.

Lots of people were arriving early. The whole town was anxious to know if the mall would be given the green light for construction. People were crowded around us as we searched for a seat. It was hot under the glare of TV-camera lights. The air was electric with tension.

There was a green-topped table where the Civic Trust members sat. Mrs. O'Neal had already taken her place at the table. She studied some notes, then glanced nervously at the crowd. Makiko and I smiled at her, and she lifted her hand in greeting.

Drake had entered and taken a seat in the audience. Colby walked in and searched the room. He waved at me, then went over and whispered something to Drake. Drake shook his head. The two seemed to argue about something. Colby's face twisted into a sneer. As I watched him, I realized I was seeing the real Colby. Even with those blue eyes, what I saw wasn't handsome.

The crowd was restless until Mrs. O'Neal called the meeting to order.

"We all know why we are here," she said. "I suggest we move directly to a vote. Mr. Walker, your vote, please."

A man rose to speak. He wore a three-piece suit and gold-rimmed spectacles. "Tonight we will decide the fate of this town," he said. "I vote yes. I'm aware of what development has done south of the border, but we need the employment. Let's build the mall, and hope for the best."

He sat down. A few people in the crowd applauded. Most watched quietly with their arms crossed. "Mrs. Ross, your vote, please."

A woman stood up from the table. She spoke bitterly against the mall. "I vote no," she said. The applause for her was loud.

The next member of the Civic Trust stood up. "I vote against." A ripple of excitement ran through the crowd. The vote continued down the table. The audience grew tense as they waited the outcome. There were three votes remaining. There was another "yes." Then another member stood. "I vote no." The crowd burst into thunderous applause. Only one more "no" vote was needed to defeat the mall. The next person stood up. "I vote yes." The crowd groaned in disappointment.

It was a tie.

It would be up to Mrs. O'Neal to decide the vote. Every eye was on her. She stood up. There was sweat on her forehead, perhaps due to the heat of the packed room. She wore a beautiful dress of emerald green. Her hair was freshly permed. She looked at her son and his wife, then at others in the crowd.

"Those of you who know me, know that this is not an easy decision for me. I've tried to be fair, to consider everyone's interest. I've listened to the arguments for both sides. Many have tried to persuade me, some with threats. But there was one group whose interest I overlooked—the young people of this town. Two remarkable young women made me aware of my oversight." She looked at me and Makiko. "The girls are here this evening."

Everyone stared at us.

Mrs. O'Neal continued. "Deciding to follow the girls' suggestion, I questioned the young people of St. Andrews. After all, we're deciding their future."

She looked at her notes.

"There are some really wonderful young people in this town. As I talked to them, I was impressed by their intelligence, and their caring. I was also amazed. I expected them to demand a mall. Instead, most wanted the Civic Trust to preserve the beauty of St. Andrews."

Mrs. O'Neal looked at her son and his wife. "I don't want you moving to Alberta with my grandchildren.

Everyone knows that. But I have to listen to my heart. I vote against the mall."

For a moment, there was a shocked silence. Then people cheered and hugged each other. It was like a New Year's Eve party! Whooping and hollering, I grabbed Makiko in a bear hug. People crowded around, shaking our hands and saying thanks for talking to Mrs. O'Neal. But not everyone was happy. Some whispered angrily to each other, and Drake stared at Mrs. O'Neal with stormy eyes. Colby ran out as soon as the vote was decided.

We managed to get through the crowd to Mrs. O'Neal, and shared a big hug. "Guess what?" she said. "I'm invited to Lethbridge for Christmas with my grandchildren. Won't that be nice? I'll see them again in only six months."

"You'll have a wonderful time," I said, hugging her again. "I really admire your courage, Mrs. O'Neal."

Makiko and I took big gulps of the cool night air once we stepped outside the courthouse. Then I stared in wonder at the sky. Hanging over the town was the moon. It was huge and glowing.

At that moment, a terrible howl filled the night. My hair stood on end. Makiko and I stared at each other, eyes huge.

"It came from the direction of Mrs. O'Neal's place," I shouted. "Come on, let's run!"

Makiko and I tore over to Mrs. O'Neal's house. We arrived in time to see flames burning near the wall of the garage. A shape lurked in the shadows near the house. In the flickering orange light, I saw a face and body thick with fur. The thing raised its head and howled. Its fangs glistened in the moonlight.

At a nearby house, someone ran onto the porch, screaming. At another house, a man yelled, "Call the cops. It's the werewolf!"

The creature ran swiftly. It crossed the lawn and ran behind a house to the nearest street. A van came from out of the darkness, turned a corner, and followed the werewolf down the same street. "It's the same van we saw at the carnival," I said.

"We should visit carnival again," Makiko replied. "And soon."

The fire was licking at the garage, moving close to the house. People were running toward Mrs. O'Neal's, carrying fire extinguishers and buckets of water. A siren sounded, moving our way fast. The fire department arrived and quickly extinguished the flames.

Makiko and I grabbed our mountain bikes and rode with all our might to the carnival.

*   *   *

The carnival lights flashed and twirled, the air boomed with music and kids screamed on the rides whirling above our heads. We hurried past the people who crowded the carnival grounds. Finding Gizmo's trailer, we slipped into the dark shadows behind it.

Cigarette smoke drifted out the open window. Creeping closer, we looked inside. Gizmo was sprawled on a kitchen chair, drinking beer. Rocky leaned against the refrigerator. He was wearing the same motorcycle gear and dusty boots, and held out a container for kerosene. "I'll get rid of this now," he said. "We won't be starting any more fires. I wouldn't want anyone finding this container."

"Don't worry," Gizmo replied. "Everyone in town thinks a werewolf caused the fires."

"And," Rocky added, "they think the werewolf lives on the island." He wiped the beer off his mouth. His moustache slipped. He fixed it, then said, "I'm going to burn the werewolf disguise." He picked it up from a heap on the floor. It had fake fur and plastic fangs.

A man hurried up to Gizmo's trailer and went inside. "Drake," I whispered. "I bet those are his goons. They tried to pressure everyone into voting yes."

Drake's voice reached us through the night. "You fools," he shouted at Gizmo and Rocky. "What are you doing? You're completely out of control."

Gizmo took a puff of his cigarette. "That fool O'Neal ignored our threats," he said. "We had to teach her a lesson."

Drake stared at him. "Who decided on the arson? I'm horrified by your actions!"

Rocky laughed. "I care this much for you," he said, snapping his fingers in Drake's face.

Gizmo slapped his hand on the table. "Give us our money. Now."

"I hired you to make sure the Civic Trust voted for the mall. I asked you to twist some arms, but I didn't expect a terror campaign! I didn't expect arson!"

Rocky's laugh was harsh. "You could have made us stop. But you were afraid the people of St. Andrews would learn the truth—that you don't have a legal claim to all the land. So, you kept quiet."

"Yes, and now I face prison." The light glowed on Drake's face. "I did a stupid thing. I was greedy, so I hired a pair of criminals to help get the mall through. Tonight, I'm going to the police. Tomorrow, when I awake, my world will be in ruins. My honor will be gone, and so will my land."

"I'd think twice about going to the police," Gizmo warned.

Drake looked at him defiantly and headed toward the door. But Rocky wasted no time. He grabbed the kerosene container and hit Drake on the head. Drake dropped to the floor.

"Tie him up. We'll deal with him later," Rocky ordered. "We have a little business to take care of on Minister's Island."

"Our chariot awaits." Gizmo gestured toward the door.

Makiko and I quickly ducked behind the trailer.

"They're heading for the van," I whispered as I watched the two men make their way through the carnival trailers in the direction of the open fields.

"We've got to move fast."

11

We entered the trailer. Drake lay on the floor, moaning. I knelt down beside him to see if he was fully conscious. His eyes looked startled.

"Liz Austen! What are you doing here?"

"Makiko and I have been working on the mystery of the St. Andrews werewolf, which led us here."

"Please untie me," Drake urged.

"Why should I? You're dangerous. You hired two thugs to pressure innocent people, burning down homes!"

"That wasn't my plan, Liz. Things were out of my control."

"Were you being blackmailed?" I asked.

"Yes. Someone in town discovered something I had thought was long forgotten."

"That you don't have a legal claim to all of the land slated for the mall. Right?"

He sighed, and slowly nodded his head. "When I made the deal, I paid off some people, so the deal was never questioned."

"But the estate you bought the land from still has a claim?"

"If people found out and someone decided to force the issue, I would probably lose all the land."

"The heir, FDR, is still alive. He could make a claim, but he doesn't know that, does he?"

"No. And the person blackmailing me was threatening to tell FDR and the entire town unless I paid him off. And the only way I could afford to pay him off was to have the mall vote go through. He was the one who forced me into hiring those two goons."

"Who *is* threatening you?"

"Colby Keaton," Drake said clearly. My heart sank. I began to tremble.

"And those guys you hired?" I managed.

Drake shrugged. "Colby's contacts. Gizmo works at the carnival, and Rocky is some friend of his. I've never seen him before."

"Maybe you know Rocky better than you think," I said.

"I don't know what you mean." Drake looked terrible, huddled on the floor.

"Just a hunch," I said. "We've got some things to take care of first, but we'll send the police to pick you up."

Makiko and I raced outside and jumped on our bikes. We both knew where we had to go next.

*　　*　　*

The kayaks were waiting for us. We jumped into them and paddled over to Minister's Island. The tide was out. The Road Beneath the Sea looked like a white ribbon on the water.

Moonlight glowed on Coven Hoven. We beached our kayaks and ran to the mansion. Gizmo's van was parked near the trees. The house was dark as we approached. "Where's everyone gone?" I whispered.

"The door is open." Makiko entered and I followed. Our footsteps echoed in the empty house. I swept the beam of my flashlight around the dark entry way. Nothing.

"Nobody's here," I said.

"What is that noise?" Makiko touched my arm. We listened for a moment. It was faint, but I could hear it—a steady *knock, knock, knock* coming from a lower bedroom.

Cautiously, we approached the closed door. The constant knocking continued. It sounded as if someone was kicking the door over and over.

Makiko stood on one side of the door, and I on the other. Quickly, I reached over and turned the knob. The door flew open. The knocking stopped. I shone my flashlight into the room.

Inside, we saw FDR, seated on the floor. He was tied up, with a gag over his mouth. Then I saw *him*. He was also tied and gagged. Now that I could see him clearly, I could tell he was no creature. But he had no ear or eyebrow, and his skin was a shiny red. His eyes were bright and intelligent. I helped him out of his ropes and extended my hand. "I'm Liz Austen. You're Lady Chandler's grandson, Wallace."

"Yes." His voice was gentle.

"You survived that terrible car crash that killed your parents."

He nodded.

"What are you doing here, FDR-san?" Makiko asked as she loosened his gag.

"I'm Wallace's tutor. I've been teaching him for years." FDR rubbed his wrists.

"That explains why I saw you here the other night," I said. "But what was in the envelope that Smart handed you?"

"My pay," FDR sighed.

"But why did you deny knowing anything about Coven Hoven?"

"I'm sorry, Liz. I was just trying to protect Wallace."

Wallace turned to us with worried eyes. "My grandmother is in trouble. Two men have taken her to the barn where we have a safe. They want to rob her. We have to help."

The night was clear as we left the mansion. The moon shone in a cloudless sky.

"I know a shortcut to the barn. This way." Wallace climbed over a fence. Makiko, FDR and I followed him as he raced across the estate toward the barn.

The barn was enormous, rising high above us. The fields all around were silver under the perfect sky. The weather vane swayed gently, as if to warn *stay away, stay away*.

I shone my flashlight on the door. The big key was in the lock, and the door was open.

We slipped in through the door. Slowly, my eyes adjusted to the darkness. I became aware of the curved roof, far above. Thick beams criss-crossed the dark air. I could smell dust—a lot of it. In the gloom, I could see piles of brittle hay, an abandoned tractor and empty stalls.

A light was on in the small office at the back of the barn. We crept over. Through the open door, we could see Rocky holding Lady Chandler. Gizmo stood in the corner, picking his teeth.

"You'll just have to be more patient. I'm an old woman." Lady Chandler was fiercely defiant. "My memory isn't as good as it used to be. I'm having trouble remembering the combination."

Rocky pulled out a knife. "Maybe this will help you remember a little better."

"You can bully all you want. I'm not afraid of your threats."

"Let's just see about that." Rocky gave a harsh laugh and brought the knife closer to her cheek. The blade glinted in the light. Lady Chandler didn't flinch.

"Leave my granny alone." Wallace left the darkness and stood in the light of the doorway. "I know the combination."

Rocky turned around, but sunglasses hid his eyes. His mouth was curled into a sneer. "If it isn't the werewolf here to save his poor granny. Welcome to the party." Rocky pointed the knife at Wallace. "Why don't you come in and open the safe?" He grabbed at Wallace as he entered the office, and pushed him roughly toward the safe.

"Run, Grandma," Wallace shouted. Rocky knocked him down. "You little liar. You don't know the combination."

Rocky raised his foot to kick Wallace.

"Stop it, Colby! Stop it right now," I shouted as I rushed into the office.

"Huh? Liz! How'd you know it was me?"

"I recognized your cologne. Besides, 'Rocky,' you almost lost your fake moustache when you were at Gizmo's."

"I told you those kids were trouble," Gizmo snarled.

"Shut up," Colby snapped at him.

"You were blackmailing Drake. You found out about the questionable land deal at the town archives, and ripped out the page, thinking you were the only one with proof. But you left enough information to make me think something was fishy." I narrowed my eyes. "You also put Drake in touch with your 'friends,' Rocky and Gizmo, so they could create a scare campaign to change the minds of the Civic Trust to vote yes."

"They needed a little persuading," Colby chuckled.

"But why did you pretend to be Rocky?" I asked.

"I like acting, and I wanted to have a little fun." Colby grinned. I was seeing the true Colby and it frightened me.

"You and Gizmo used the legend of the St. Andrews werewolf to your own ends. You brought it alive with a costume."

"It looked pretty convincing, don't you think?"

"Then you tried to put the blame on FDR. You wanted people to think he was the arsonist, so you called him and told him to go to the Algonquin Hotel. Then you broke into his house and left a fake note for us."

"Yes. And I got you to arrive at the hotel in time to see the werewolf setting the fire. I wanted you to suspect FDR."

"Well, you forgot one thing," I said evenly.

"What's that, Sherlock Holmes?" Colby taunted.

"FDR is right-handed. The note I found was written by a southpaw. The writing slanted to the back. You're a lefty, aren't you, Colby?"

"Very clever."

"You also told me the carnival opened at dusk, but it opens at noon. You invited us sailing so we wouldn't search for the van. And I just bet you phoned Gizmo from the pier to tell him to hide the van."

"You're a smart girl, Liz. You figured everything out. But what are you going to do about it?"

"Tell the police."

"Do you think I'm going to let you leave here?" Colby asked as he moved toward me.

"Stop right there, Colby. You're outnumbered." FDR and Makiko came into the office.

Colby laughed, more like a snort. "By what? A werewolf, an old lady, a wimp and two girls? Give me a break!"

"Why don't you add an old man with a shotgun."

We all turned around to see Smart standing in the doorway, pointing a gun. "Drop the knife."

Gizmo raised his hands in the air. Before anyone could do anything, Colby grabbed me and placed the knife at my throat. "Don't anybody move, or she's toast."

Keeping the knife at my throat, Colby edged me toward the door. "Stay where you are, and she doesn't get hurt. Liz and I are getting out of here."

"What about me?" Gizmo cried.

"Every man for himself." Colby pushed me out of the office, through the barn and outside into the evening air.

"You won't get away with this, Colby. Drake will tell the police everything."

"Well, they'll have to chase both of us, then, won't they?" Colby dragged me across the estate until we came to Gizmo's van. Inside was Colby's motorcycle.

"Get on in front," Colby ordered once the bike was out of the van. I climbed on. Colby sat behind me. He put the knife in his pocket. His arms went around me as he reached for the handle bars. With one big kick, he started the motorcycle. The Harley raced off, heading for the Road Beneath the Sea.

We soon reached the water's edge. The Road Beneath the Sea was still visible, but the tide was beginning to rise. I heard it gurgling and *shlooping* around the rocks. "We'll never make it!" I screamed.

"We'll have to try." Colby turned his powerful bike onto the road and headed off toward the mainland. He leaned forward, causing me to bend. He was trying to outrace the tide.

Halfway out on the road, the bike stopped. The head-lights glittered on the water covering the road ahead of us. I looked behind us and saw only darkness. We were a long way from shore.

"We're trapped," I cried. "The water's surrounding us."

Colby and I jumped off the bike and the water swirled around our knees. "We're going to die," Colby blubbered. He was paralyzed with fear.

"You're pathetic," I snorted. I tried to think fast. How could we get to shore?

I heard the sound of something coming up behind us. I turned around. Coming through the night on his white stallion was Wallace.

"Jump on, Liz," Wallace called as he rode up. I pulled myself up behind him.

"What about me?" Colby cried.

"Give me your knife first," I called down to him.

When it was in my hand, Colby scrambled onto the horse. He was shaking in terror.

Wallace turned the horse around and urged him toward Minister's Island. We went as fast as we could along the roadway. We were getting closer to the island, but the stallion was having difficulty. The water was deeper, the currents stronger and we were heavy.

The stallion stopped moving. It nervously examined

the water rushing past. I was getting scared. Wallace nudged the horse with his heels, and it cautiously moved forward.

The water pressed against the horse's chest. I could see the shoreline ahead. Wallace urged the stallion, "You can do it! You're a beautiful horse, you're a champion."

The stallion whinnied. He struggled forward. Colby cried out in horror as the horse stumbled. The water roared around us, pulling at the stallion, but somehow he battled forward. At last he stumbled free of the currents, and stepped onto the island.

Lady Chandler and the others were waiting for us. Smart was there with his shotgun. He took control of Colby. I gave Makiko a hug of relief.

The police came in motor boats and arrested Gizmo and Colby. They took us home, too, and I told them where to find Drake.

It had been a long night.

*   *   *

The next morning, Fran had some important news for me. "I've heard from Emily's mother. She phoned to thank you, Liz."

"For what?"

"Emily was being abused by her stepfather, and she broke her silence yesterday. The person she told went straight to the authorities."

I was shocked. "Emily has so much courage."

"I'm sure it was difficult for her. But you know what?" Fran put her arm around my shoulder.

"What?" I said, looking up at her.

"Emily's mom says that you and Makiko have been such good friends to Emily. So supportive. That kind of positive feeling made Emily feel good about herself. Good enough to make her realize she didn't deserve the treatment she was getting. I'm proud of you girls."

"What's going to happen now?" I asked quietly.

"I'm not sure, but she's going to need some real good friends."

I nodded my head. Emily could count on me.

"And how do *you* feel this morning, Liz?" Fran looked concerned.

"I'm glad that everything is working out and that St. Andrews is back to normal. But I've realized you were right about something."

"What's that?"

"Remember, after the Canada Day celebrations, you told me to look beneath the surface—get to know people by what's inside?"

"Yes."

"Well, Colby Keaton really fooled me. I thought he was a good person, and it frightens me that it took so long to find out the truth."

"You have to trust your instincts, Liz. Your inner voice will guide you." Fran hugged me close.

*　　　*　　　*

We had only one more dress rehearsal before the opening night. That afternoon, I hurried to the theater. Makiko was already in her usual place in the audience. I waved to her from the stage. She gave me the thumbs up sign.

I hurried toward my dressing room. On my way, I saw Emily sitting by herself. I went over and put my arms around her. "I'm so proud of you, Emily. You were really brave."

Emily nodded. Her face was sad. "I'm not going to be in the play," she said.

"Why? You've worked so hard. You love this play."

Emily nodded. "But people will know I'm bad."

"No, Emily," I said gently. "People know that he's bad. Nobody thinks you're bad."

"I can't go on stage."

"He hurt you. Don't let him destroy what you love."

Emily sat quietly. I gave her a hug. "It must be so hard for you. It took courage to do what you did. I'm so proud of you." Emily nodded. A tear trickled down her cheek.

"I can understand that you don't want to go on stage. But it makes me sad," I said, "because I know you have the courage."

Emily smiled. "Thanks, Liz," she said quietly.

*　　*　　*

The next day, I was *exceptionally* nervous. It was opening night for our musical. I kept taking deep breaths as I applied makeup. Stuck to the mirror was a telegram from my family. I'd also received flowers.

There were flowers in all the dressing rooms, and the doors were covered with cards that said *break a leg*.

"Enjoy the show," Colin smiled, handing envelopes to Barbara and me. He'd written everyone a personal note. We'd all worked really hard in extra rehearsals with the understudies who'd stepped in to replace Colby and Drake, who were both in custody, along with Gizmo.

Miss Hannigan was applying number 5 greasepaint. "I hear Lady Chandler has asked FDR to help turn Coven Hoven into a kids' center."

"That's right," I said. "Kids from all over the world will have fun together on Minister's Island, and experts will attend conferences to discuss issues involving children. Mrs. O'Neal's son will be working on the project, so her grandchildren won't be leaving town. And FDR will start a claim for the right to his property. He wants to fulfill his dream and donate the land to St. Andrews for use as a park."

Above us in the dressing room was a black-and-white TV set. The TV showed the theater curtain. We could hear coughs from the audience as the orchestra warmed up. My stomach was clenched tight.

After the overture, the curtain rose. On the TV, we could see the iron beds where the orphans were sleeping. One of them was Emily—I knew she'd do the show! The tiniest girl, Molly, clutched a teddy with ragged ears as she looked into the spotlight and began the show's opening song, "Maybe."

It was a hit! The audience cheered the orphans, then they cheered the next songs and the dancing and the sets. They loved it all. On stage, I basked in the laughter and the waves of applause rolling out of the crowd.

During intermission, everyone stood around together in the dressing rooms, talking excitedly. Some parents came from the audience, bringing rave reviews. I saw Emily hugging her mother, and went to say hello.

"Isn't it exciting?" Emily exclaimed. "I love being in this show."

"I'm so proud of Emily," her mother said. "We're living on our own now, Liz. We're getting help from support agencies and there's been a court order—my husband has to stay away from us."

"I get sad sometimes," Emily said, "but it seems a bit better every day. I'm joining a counselling group in September. My social worker arranged it. I like her." She put her arms around me. "But you're my best friend, Liz. Always."

Her mother smiled. "We're doing lots of hugging these days. I need them, too."

*   *   *

The second act of *Annie* passed far too quickly. I was swept up in the adventure, and wished it would last forever. Our curtain calls were wonderful—the crowd was on its feet cheering as once again we sang the hit song, "Tomorrow." *This is great*, I thought, waving at Makiko in the audience.

Wallace was there with his grandmother and Smart. After the play, they came backstage. Wallace handed me a bouquet of flowers. "You were wonderful," he smiled.

"Thanks," I blushed.

Lady Chandler shook my hand. "I was so wrong about keeping Wallace away from the world. You made me see my mistakes. I was afraid, you see. Afraid that people would be cruel. I just wanted to protect him."

"You were trying your best, grandma." Wallace looked at her. "I was afraid, too. Afraid of what people might see. I didn't want them laughing at me. But people have been nice."

"Well, I hope my plans for a children's center at Coven Hoven can help me make it up to the people of St. Andrews and to Wallace."

At that moment, Emily rushed toward me and gave me a huge hug.

"See, you *do* have courage," I said, smiling proudly. "Know what's the best? You've set yourself free."

ABOUT THE AUTHOR

As part of his research for this book, Eric Wilson appeared in *Annie* as Judge Brandeis when the musical was performed in his home town of Victoria, B.C. He is seen here with others from the cast.

Eric's research also included consulting with specialists in the field of child sexual abuse. He read many books on the topic, and was deeply moved by the experiences of the children who speak in the pages of *Am I the Only One?*, edited by Dennis Foon and Brenda Knight. If you want to know more, ask for the book at your local library or bookstore.

THE PRAIRIE DOG CONSPIRACY

A Tom Austen Mystery

Eric Wilson

. . . for a moment there was silence. Then a gunshot rang out. It echoed down the river valley, followed by a cry of horror. Tom stared in disbelief as a body tumbled from the train and fell toward the river.

During a long cold winter in his home town of Winnipeg, Tom stumbles across some strange activity in an abandoned house. With the reluctant help of his friend Dietmar Oban, Tom finds himself chasing false leads and ends up in the middle of something more dangerous than he suspected. Through the snowy streets of Winnipeg, aboard the historic *Prairie Dog Central* and during a Ski Doo chase beneath the Northern Lights, Tom unravels the secret of "the Golden Child" and in the process realizes that the safety of one of his friends depends on him.

THE ICE DIAMOND QUEST

A Tom and Liz Austen Mystery

Eric Wilson

As a flare lit the night, the sea turned crimson. In the bright light, they saw a powerful yacht. On its bridge, a signal light began to flash.

Why is this mysterious yacht flashing a signal off the coast of Newfoundland on a cold November evening? Tom and Liz Austen, with their cousins Sarah and Duncan Joy, follow a difficult trail toward the truth. As they search, people known as the Hawk and the Renegades cause major problems, but the cousins press on. Then, in the darkness of an abandoned mine and later on stormy seas, they face together the greatest dangers ever.

COLD MIDNIGHT IN VIEUX QUÉBEC

A Tom Austen Mystery

Eric Wilson

Fireworks exploded into the sky above the Ice Palace as Tom struggled forward through the throngs of people, then was suddenly grabbed by a big police officer.
  "Tu ne peux pas aller là-bas. *That is a security zone.*"
  "You've got to let me get past," Tom shouted.

The leaders of the world's superpowers have agreed to meet in Québec City to put an end to chemical weapons — but powerful forces will stop at nothing to prevent the agreement from being signed. From the first chilling page, you will be gripped by suspense as you follow Tom Austen and Dietmar Oban through the ancient, mysterious streets of Vieux Québec in quest of world peace.

CODE RED AT THE SUPERMALL

A Tom and Liz Austen Mystery

Eric Wilson

They swam past gently moving strands of seaweed and pieces of jagged coral, then Tom almost choked in horror. A shark was coming straight at him, ready to strike.

Have you ever visited a shopping mall that has sharks and piranhas, a triple-loop rollercoaster, 22 waterslides, an Ice Palace, submarines, 828 stores, and a major mystery to solve? Soon after Tom and Liz Austen arrive at the West Edmonton Mall, a bomber strikes and they must follow a trail that leads through the fabled splendors of the supermall to hidden danger.

THE GREEN GABLES DETECTIVES

A Liz Austen Mystery

Eric Wilson

I almost expected to see Anne signalling to Diana from her bedroom window as we climbed the slope towards Green Gables, then Makiko grabbed my arm. "Danger!"

Staring at the house, I saw a dim shape slip around a corner into hiding. "Who's there?" I called. "We see you!"

While visiting the famous farmhouse known as Green Gables, Liz Austen and her friends are swept up in baffling events that lead from an ancient cemetery to a haunted church, and then a heart-stopping showdown in a deserted lighthouse as fog swirls across Prince Edward Island. Be prepared for eerie events and unbearable suspense as you join the Green Gables detectives for a thrilling adventure.

SPIRIT IN THE RAINFOREST

A Tom and Liz Austen Mystery

Eric Wilson

The branches trembled, then something slipped away into the darkness of the forest. "That was Mosquito Joe!" Tom exclaimed.

"Or his spirit," Liz said. "Let's get out of here."

The rainforest of British Columbia holds many secrets, but none stranger than those of Nearby Island. After hair-raising events during a Pacific storm, Tom and Liz Austen seek answers among the island's looming trees. Alarmed by the ghostly shape of the hermit Mosquito Joe, they look for shelter in a deserted school in the rainforest. Then, in the night, Tom and Liz hear a girl's voice crying *Beware! Beware!*

VAMPIRES OF OTTAWA

A Liz Austen Mystery

Eric Wilson

Suddenly the vampire rose up from behind a tombstone and fled, looking like an enormous bat with his black cape streaming behind in the moonlight.

Within the walls of a gloomy estate known as Blackwater, Liz Austen discovers the strange world of Baron Nicolai Zaba, a man who lives in constant fear. What is the secret of the ancient chapel's underground vault? Why are the words *In Evil Memory* scrawled on a wall? Who secretly threatens the Baron? All the answers lie within these pages but be warned: *reading this book will make your blood run cold.*

THE KOOTENAY KIDNAPPER

A Tom Austen Mystery

Eric Wilson

Only groans and creaks sounded from the old building as it waited for Tom to discover its secret. With a rapidly-beating heart, he approached the staircase ...

What is the secret lurking in the ruins of the lonely ghost town in the mountains of British Columbia? Solving this mystery is only one of the challenges facing Tom Austen after he arrives in B.C. with his sidekick, Dietmar Oban, and learns that a young girl has disappeared without a trace. Then a boy is kidnapped, and electrifying events quickly carry Tom to a breathtaking climax deep underground in Cody Caves, where it is forever night ...